KOREAN SHORT STORIES

**A COLLECTION
FROM NORTH KOREA**

Fredonia Books
Amsterdam, The Netherlands

Korean Short Stories:
A Collection from North Korea

ISBN: 1-4101-0218-1

Copyright © 2003 by Fredonia Books

Reprinted from the original edition

Fredonia Books
Amsterdam, The Netherlands
http://www.fredoniabooks.com

All rights reserved, including the right to reproduce this book, or portions thereof, in any form.

CONTENTS

HISTORY OF IRON
                Pyon Hui Gun 2

HAPPINESS
                Sok Yun Gi 30

OGI
                Chon Se Bong 71

FELLOW TRAVELLERS
                Kim Byong Hun 100

EVERYONE IN POSITION!
                Om Dan Ung 132

UNFINISHED SCULPTURE
                Ko Byong Sam 152

History of Iron

Pyon Hui Gun

It was three days after the ceasefire.

The milky morning mist was hovering over the ironworks which had been severely damaged by the shells and bombs of the three years' war. There was dead silence in the compound of scattered broken bricks and rusty scrap iron.

A shadow appeared in the mist in front of the coke oven shop whose roof and walls had been blown off. The worker wore faded grey overalls and a white cap. He had several days' growth of grey whiskers on his hollow cheeks: clearly he was well over fifty. His duck shoes and the bottoms of his trousers were wet probably from walking in dewy grass.

He walked slowly, bending forward looking for something. When he found a half-buried nut he stopped, picked it up, scraped the dirt off it and threw it into the sack that hung from his shoulders. He moved on. His name was Pak Ung Chil. He was an old furnace builder.

When he reached the wire shop, he sat down beside the broken wall to roll a cigarette. He took a rest and smoked it.

A light brackish breeze blew over from the Taedong River. A thick morning mist moved onward towards Mt.

Wolbong—reluctantly, sick from lack of sleep. Traces of the American imperialist gang's crimes came to light through the mist one by one, gnawing at his heart.

The rusty dead blast furnace, the bent, crooked steel skeletons of open-hearth furnaces, the crumbling walls of the rolling shop, zigzag gas pipes and tubes lying topsy-turvy on the ground, broken chimneys....

Ung Chil's eyes burned with anger boiling up with hatred for the Yanks.

"Bloody swine!"

Ung Chil clenched his teeth. The hard days of the war rose uninvited before his eyes.

The day when they had made melted iron plates by building bullet-proof walls around the blast furnaces, the open-hearth furnaces and machines to protect them against enemy raids; the time when they reluctantly retreated with vital machine pieces on their backs after removing larger machines to the mountain for safety; the day they set up small blast furnaces underground to make war materials from melted iron for the front.... Endless recollections. But the most poignant was the separation from Byong Du with whom he had worked for twenty years.

Five enemy planes were shot down by our anti-aircraft guns that day, but instead of giving up, the enemy made further raids.

The steel in the open-hearth furnaces was ready to flow out boiling when there was the first raid. Parts of the ceilings of furnaces No. 1 and No. 3 were falling in with the blast of nearby bombs. Fire leaked out so that they could not hold their heat, which meant losing a load of steel that should be made into guns to fight the enemy.

Neither Ung Chil nor Byong Du could bear the thought.

For a moment their eyes met and they understood each other. Ung Chil climbed up on furnace No. 1, Byong Du ran to No. 3.

Their battle began: they used iron hooks to try to fill in holes with fire bricks from which the flames shot out at them.

The smelters watched their magnificent struggle in great excitement.

The wild flames attacked as if they might consume them any

moment, but they took no heed. The fight went ahead in hushed silence.

The mad flames began to recede before their undaunted spirit.

Ung Chil finished filling in his gaping. He wiped the sweat from his face with the back of his hand, and turned to furnace No. 3, where Byong Du, too, having finished his work, turned grinning to Ung Chil.

At that moment came the second wave of enemy planes and bombs began to rain down on the roof of the steel-ingot shop that was ready to receive the molten steel.

A loud roar filled the shop.

The blast shook Ung Chil. He grabbed the steel skeleton next to him and threw himself down on the furnace, facing Byong Du. Byong Du twisted, staggered and fell. Ung Chil started up crying "Byong Du!" and jumped down to the floor.

Other smelters had already got up on the furnace top; now they were coming down carrying Byong Du. Bomb splinters had caught him in the back and blood was seeping from his overalls. The smelters carried him straight to the hospital.

Byong Du was seriously wounded. But the next morning he said to Ung Chil: "Hullo, Ung Chil.... We promised to produce iron from the reconstructed furnace to the end of our lives true to our leader's teaching, didn't we?... But I... am sorry, indeed.... Please take vengeance... upon the enemy. Our leader will certainly visit our works when we discharge the first molten iron.... Will you give him my best regards? Our leader... our leader will remember me, I'm sure.... I am sorry indeed that I shall not be able to work under his warm care for many more years...."

With these words he breathed his last.

Now Ung Chil remembered the face of Byong Du who stared at him eagerly with his moist eyes as if he was complaining of his departure with many stories untold from this world, and Ung Chil's heart was bursting with grief.

"How splendid it would be if Byong Du were alive!"

Ung Chil's face covered in wrinkles and grey whiskers looked woebegone.

"Do you know something in your grave, Byong Du? We've defeated the Yankees.... Soon we'll rebuild the furnace to produce iron and have the leader coming here."

Ung Chil felt as though he was making the promise to the dead Byong Du.

But how to begin? In his anxiety to rebuild the works he had again come out very early to collect up old nuts and bolts, though the prospect of rebuilding was remote.

Neither unbroken bricks nor nuts and bolts were readily available, and how could they get the quantities of iron or cement, or indeed the workers and technicians? Deep sorrow took over him. He thought about it sadly as he started out, his sack slung over his shoulder.

He was coming up to the road, when he saw some people moving in front of the open-hearth furnace shop which was still covered with mist.

"Who could they be so early in this morning?"

Walking up to them with a mystified air Ung Chil cried, "Who there?"

"It's me," a loud voice sounded after a while. Ung Chil was struck. The voice was so familiar. A thought flashed across his mind. But he rejected his improbable idea saying to himself: "What a delusion I'm nursing!" and hurriedly walked in that direction.

As soon as the man in weekday clothes became visible through the mist Ung Chil stopped short. Completely shaken he stared in disbelief.

He couldn't trust his own eyes. It was Marshal Kim Il Sung.

Ung Chil did not know how to behave, it was so sudden and unexpected.

Who could imagine that he would be here so early in the morning?

However hard the days of war were, however bitter the conditions, he always dwelt in his heart. Ung Chil was encouraged and fully assured of our victory because the leader had showed the way. And now he was near him, stepping towards him!

Suddenly Ung Chil choked and his eyes grew dim. Meanwhile the leader approached Ung Chil.

"Excuse me for entering without permission from the masters," he said. Then, taking a closer look at Ung Chil he

went on, "Well, who are you? Isn't it Comrade Ung Chil?" he was rather surprised.

"Yes, it is me, dear leader! I'm the furnace builder Ung Chil," Ung Chil could hardly control his tears.

"Certainly! It is you. What hard time you have had during the war? I missed you badly even in these hard times. I'm truly glad to see you!"

Smiling, the leader grasped Ung Chil's hand, his face beaming.

Tears that were hardly checked before streamed down Ung Chil's wrinkled cheeks.

"Dear leader! Now I am..."

"Well, are you wounded? Is your family all right?" the leader asked.

"Yes, they are all right."

"How are you getting along? I am sure you must be in need."

"We are well-off, under the care of the Party."

"Why, of course, you must have needs, for there was a war.... Wait a little. We shall overcome. Everything will be better soon. Now, what have you in your sack?"

Ung Chil came to himself. He had a sack hung over his shoulder! He was puzzled.

"They are nuts and bolts found in the compound.... Thinking that they may be useful when the reconstruction starts." The leader stared at Ung Chil in silence.

"I see. How is Comrade Byong Du?" he asked.

Ung Chil couldn't answer at first. He feared the leader would feel heartsore if he heard of Byong Du's death.

The leader guessed and asked, "Was there an accident... do you say?"

"Yes, when he was fixing the hole in the top of the open-hearth furnace during an air raid...." Ung Chil hung his head.

The leader's face darkened.

Ung Chil looked up again and told the leader what had happened:

"Byong Du asked me to give you his best regards when you visit here to see the first molten iron from the reconstructed furnace, dear leader. He said he was sorry that he couldn't work under your warm care for many more years...."

The leader quickly turned his face away looking up at the sky with moist eyes.

"We have lost a fine comrade. He was about fifty-four, wasn't he?" the leader asked in a quiet tone.

"Yes, he was."

"Fifty-four! He was in the noon of life.... But without seeing the brighter days...."

The leader became silent for a few moments and then gently said: "Where are his family now?"

"In Cholsan-ri. His wife lives with her youngest son and daughter. His eldest son who was a smelter, too, and his second son are both at the front."

"Let's visit them afterwards. Bereaved of her husband, she may be badly off. Let's help them for Byong Du and his sons at the front. The young ones will be sent to the Revolution School.... Now Comrade Ung Chil! Meeting you here, I remember the day when we discharged molten iron for the first time after liberation. I'm sure you went after Comrade Byong Du to bring him back when he was returning to his birthplace because of the difficulties immediately after liberation, didn't you?"

"Yes, I did."

"We had a hard struggle in those days, too."

The leader said this as if to himself, lost in thought, and quietly stepped up towards the entrance of the open-hearth furnace shop.

Following him Ung Chil vividly recalled the days when under his guidance, they had started to reconstruct the iron and steel works which the fleeing Japs had destroyed....

The whole country was boiling like a cauldron with the excitement of liberation.

Ung Chil had greeted liberation at the steel works. The Japs had broken the converters without taking out the steel, and running for it, bragged that the Koreans would not be able to operate them even in twenty years.

It was certain that they would enjoy a better life after liberation. But factories were shut and the workers had to fight their way through great hardship for a time. So some workers stayed at home doing odd jobs to earn bread, while others left the works for their own towns or villages hoping for some windfall. The overwhelming majority of conscious workers, however, organized the guards to defend and to rebuild the works. Ung Chil had joined the guards together with Byong Du. But Byong Du had a bigger family so that inevitably his life was the harder.

One evening Byong Du dropped in and said to Ung Chil abruptly:

"I'd rather go back to my native village."

"Do you really mean it?" Ung Chil was surprised.

He had never thought that Byong Du would make such a decision. He knew the life of Byong Du who, thrown off his land by the landlord at Cholwon, Kangwon Province, became a labourer.

"How could I want to leave the works? But in the present conditions it would be better to follow the plow."

"Do you hope to get land there?"

"Never! I only count on my wife's parents there."

"What a fool! Your land was taken by your landlord and you've become a labourer... besides that how can you go back home in such rags? You are really poor-spirited." Ung Chil spoke roughly to him.

"Well, then, what is there for me to do here? We are furnace builders, right? When can we get a job? The Japanese imperialists damaged the furnaces so badly. Can I sit down like a fool and watch dead furnaces?"

For this Ung Chil could find no answer.

Unless he found Byong Du a job it would be impossible to make him stay, however regretfully he went. His heart ached at the thought of separation from his old friend.

"Won't you wait a bit more? They say life will become better..." he advised.

A few days after that the Byong Dus left for their native village.

The two families parted in tears.

After seeing the Byong Dus off, Ung Chil went to the works. From habit his legs carried him to the converter shop.

The shop was as silent as death.

Everything seemed unfamiliar there, but again from habit he went over to the furnace and looked in. The molten metal had congealed in it. Once again his hatred against the Japanese imperialists flared up.

"When will we discharge molten steel?"

Close by the furnace he missed Byong Du all the more.

The talk in the town about General Kim Il Sung was brought to his mind.

As soon as the country was liberated the people unanimously wished General Kim Il Sung to administer the affairs of state. Wasn't he the peerless patriot and national hero whom they longed for so ardently in the dark days when they were trampled underfoot by the Japanese imperialists?

When he administers the affairs of state all the poor will enjoy freedom and happiness and he will build a wealthy and strong state. That was the firm conviction of our people.

Rumour spread at the time that General Kim Il Sung had returned to Pyongyang and visited some factories. Ung Chil's steelworks heard of it, too. The workers were greatly excited hoping that he would come to their works. Whenever anyone came from Pyongyang they would run up to him expecting to hear such news.

"How happy we would be if General Kim Il Sung visited our works! But that is impossible, for he is so busy...."

Thus Ung Chil was musing, when a loud voice sounded at the back, "Hullo, how are you?"

Ung Chil was surprised. Behind him was a tall, finely-built stranger followed by a medium-sized man. The tall man's eyes sparkled with vitality.

Ung Chil noted a dignified something in his bearing.

"Where are you from?" he asked timidly.

"We dropped in to see the works on our way to another place." The guest answered, smiling. Once his smile played upon his lips the dignified appearance suddenly changed to a mild humour. Ung Chil's heart thawed.

"What can you expect from the works which is more dead than alive?" he asked.

"Is the works being badly damaged?" the guest said turning his eyes to the compound of the works.

"Yes, almost completely wrecked. Look at that furnace. The villains escaped after demolishing the furnace without taking out the molten steel. Now I have no job. I was a furnace builder for more than fifteen years." Ung Chil sighed.

The guest became serious. He looked into the furnace. His eyes flashed.

"The Japanese imperialists are cunning by nature," he said sonorously.

Judging from the guest's character and behaviour Ung Chil concluded that he was well informed about the world.

"I want to ask you just one thing..." Ung Chil said, "There are rumours that General Kim Il Sung has returned to Pyongyang—is it true?"

The guest gave him a meaningful look and said: "Ha! ha!—well, why do you ask about it?"

"Because I have a feeling of impatience. They say we workers will be free only when he administers the affairs of state. Whom else can we expect but him? Even three-year-old children knew about him from the time the Japanese imperialists ruled. The workers here are anxious to see him once.... Suppose they leave the works one after another. I'm afraid the works will be shut down forever just as the Japanese wished."

Ung Chil clicked his tongue showing his disappointment that the guests could not give him any news about General Kim Il Sung.

"Are there many abandoning the works?"

"Quite a few. This morning I saw off a friend named Byong Du. I'm left by the partner who worked with me through thick and thin at various places, I'm really sorry about that. In furnace building there are very few to match him," Ung Chil sighed once again.

"That may happen, for they are so poor. But the workers should not abandon the works, should they?"

The guest studying Ung Chil's face quietly admonished.

"What are we to do then when there isn't any job?... If we had a job, we wouldn't quit, not even if someone tried to lock us out."

"Why no job? In my opinion every nook of the works is full of things to be done." The guest went on in a low but majestic tone. "The masters of the works now are not the Japanese imperialists but the workers."

"What? You say the workers are the masters of the works?" Ung Chil asked dubiously.

"Yes, they are, How did the Japanese imperialists build the

works? Didn't they squeeze blood and sweat from the workers to build it? Workers ought to take everything back. And workers and peasants who were poverty-stricken in the past must build their own country into a happy society."

This seemed interesting to Ung Chil.

"It would be nice if such a country could be built. It seems to me like a dream."

"Why do you think it's a dream? Such a country will certainly be built. But, for that, the workers have to stay in the works and be fine masters of it. From now on the entire works is the property of the country and the workers. How can the masters who should be defending the property leave? That means resigning their right of managing their own property."

"Quite true! I understand now. We confined ourselves only to furnace building and never tried to understand the world better," Ung Chil was ashamed of his lack of knowledge.

But while listening to the guest he felt he saw the world far more clearly.

"Who is this who knows the world so well and calls the workers masters of the country?"

Suddenly Ung Chil recalled the rumours saying that General Kim Il Sung who returned home had already visited a factory, and thought: "Could he be General Kim Il Sung?"

The guest said that knowledge was power and that, to be masters of the works, workers should be versed in politics and know how to operate the works. He said that in the past the Japanese imperialists let Koreans do only physical labour lest they should learn techniques, but now that the country had been liberated they could learn anything if they wanted to.

"We must start operating the works and produce iron as early as possible. Without iron we can neither build the country nor improve the people's living," said he and went on:

"Look! If we are to reconstruct the works destroyed by Japs, build houses and make machines to weave cloth, we have to produce iron.

"Why were we robbed of our country by the Japanese imperialists? When they bustled themselves making guns and warships, producing iron to raid us, our rulers were singing the praises of profound peace on a donkey's back and putting on a horsehair hat.

"Not surprising we were conquered?... We must not follow in their wake. We should produce iron ourselves, arm the army and annihilate the aggressors in one blow. Iron is all important! The masters of these works, too, must produce iron as soon as possible."

Ung Chil felt a new strength welling up in his body. But he was quite puzzled over the question of operating the works.

"To produce iron someone has to run the works. But this is quite beyond our power...," he mumbled to himself.

"Of course it is not simple. But there is nothing impossible in this world for workers. For instance, do not factories, machines, buildings, guns, aeroplanes, warships... come from the wisdom and strength of workers? If workers are united they can succeed in everything. Don't hesitate but be bold. Then we will be able to operate the works soon and produce iron by ourselves."

After this encouragement the guest took his leave.

"O! Are you leaving so soon?"

Ung Chil was sorry. He wanted to learn more from him.

"Yes, I must leave. We'll meet again. What is your name?"

"I'm Pak Ung Chil, I've learned much from you, dear guest," Ung Chil said politely.

"Not at all. I've learned a lot from what you said. I will be looking forward to the day when iron will flow out from these works. Good-bye," said he and shook hands with Ung Chil.

Ung Chil stood there with an abstracted air till the guest went out of the gate.

He felt he knew more and understood what action had to be taken in such confusion and disorder. He began to entertain a hope that the man was possibly General Kim Il Sung himself. "Why didn't I ask him his name? Shall I go after him and ask?..." But he dared not. He turned to the back gate of the works and went home.

His wife was out with the children. The hope haunted him all the more, and every word the guest spoke came to his mind vividly.

After a while his wife ran up to him out of breath from outside.

"What a happy event it is?"

"Why all the noise?" Ung Chil glanced at her without any interest.

"Why! General Kim Il Sung about whom you talked so often visited the works today. It's the talk of the town."

"What!" Ung Chil started up. "Is it t—true?"

"Why would I make up such a story, if it were not true? People are so excited.... They say that their lives will begin improving from tomorrow."

"Is there anyone who saw him?"

"Yes, uncle Sun Taek and uncle Dok Man did."

Ung Chil slapped his knee: "I was right! He was General Kim Il Sung!"

Being a man of action, Ung Chil could not waste time in small talk. He ran up to sheet metal worker Dok Man.

Fortunately Dok Man happened to be home.

"Hey, Dok Man! Is it true that you met General Kim Il Sung?" Ung Chil asked abruptly.

"Sure! I never expected to meet him so early," he answered exultantly.

"I was in the sheet-metal processing shop putting things in order with Sun Taek, when the outside was agog with excitement. I came out and found the yard in front of the office was crowded with people. All of them raised their hands crying 'Long live General Kim Il Sung!'

"We ran up to them without knowing what it was all about. A tall finely-built guest was on the step of the porch with the cadres of the works' guards, and they said that he was the great leader General Kim Il Sung. I was deeply touched and shouted hurrah for him. The General said that we workers were the masters of the works from now on and that we should guard the works well. I could not keep back my tears...."

Dok Man mopped the corner of his eye.

Ung Chil asked Dok Man to describe the General in detail.

From the answer he was certain that it was General Kim Il Sung he had met.

"What a great mistake I made!" Ung Chil said to himself, feeling a lump in his throat.

"Well!... What's the matter?" Dok Man asked Ung Chil dubiously.

"What did he think about me? I chattered about anything

and everything indiscreetly?"

"Have you seen him, too?" Dok Man was surprised.

"I have. Perhaps I was the first man in the works to see him. But I'm afraid I made a big mistake...."

Ung Chil left Dok Man's. He felt embarrassed for his indiscretion. On his way he saw a crowd proceeding towards the office. He thought he would go in that direction, but just then he heard the hammering of sheet metal from smelter Hui Su's yard which was encircled with maize. It was certain that Hui Su was cutting sheet metal for buckets. Ung Chil changed his mind about going to the office—abruptly he walked into Hui Su's yard. As he expected Hui Su was marking sheet metal with a piece of chalk.

"Hullo, Hui Su! How long are you going to do this?" Ung Chil cried sternly staring at him.

"What else can I do when the works is closed?" Hui Su glanced at Ung Chil.

"Well, don't you know that General Kim Il Sung visited our works?"

"What? General Kim Il Sung?" Hui Su opened his eyes in wonder. He pushed aside the sheet metal and asked: "Is it true, uncle?"

"Hum! You waste your time making buckets and don't know what is happening outside!..." Ung Chil squatted down. Hui Su sat down beside him awkwardly.

"You must be discreet hereafter," Ung Chil said and began telling him how he met General Kim Il Sung and what he was instructed.

Hui Su was excited, even tears appeared in his eyes.

"Do you think, Hui Su, we can carry on the way we did instead of defending the works as General Kim Il Sung wished?" Ung Chil admonished.

"Uncle Ung Chil, I'm sorry. I was wrong, I will come to the works every day from now on," Hui Su said, blushing.

"Well, let's go at once!" Ung Chil pulled Hui Su by the sleeve.

After a while Ung Chil and Hui Su were running toward the office at the works where people were gathering.

Ung Chil was awake till late that night. The faces of those who cried and shook their fists demanding to reconstruct the works at once as General Kim Il Sung instructed flashed across his mind one after another.

They were as spirited as the rolling waves which had been once stagnant missing their course, and now encouraged by him, dashed forth. The more he thought, the more everything seemed to be a dream.

The workers had looked up to General Kim Il Sung like a lighthouse ever since the dark days when the Japanese imperialists used bayonets to keep them down. General Kim Il Sung had defeated the enemy and liberated the fatherland! Ung Chil was very glad to see him and could hardly control his excitement.

The case of "pumpkin heads" came to his mind for which Byong Du and himself had been taken to the police station and tortured for one month and a half.

When Byong Du had gone to the Songjin High Frequency Works he had heard an episode of "pumpkin heads" from his friends. The Japanese troops from Ranam and Hamhung surged to "mop up" General Kim Il Sung's unit. But they were annihilated by the brilliant tactics of General Kim Il Sung. And the Japanese, unable to carry their numberless bodies, cut off heads from the bodies and packed them into jute bags to carry secretly on ox-carts. A driver who knew the secret, pretending ignorance, asked indifferently "What are they?" The Japanese private answered: "They are... pumpkins, you fool!" In those days the talk that General Kim Il Sung used magic tactics and ran as a flash of lightning from east to west or in the opposite direction cutting a hundred miles to mow down the Japanese soldiers was so widely circulated that the episode of "pumpkin heads," too, soon spread among the workers. And the whole works buzzed like a stirred-up beehive.

The police arrested workers at random trying to find a source of information. Byong Du and Ung Chil, too, were arrested.

The police tortured them, saying that they had invented the whole story. But Ung Chil never lost courage, and thought about General Kim Il Sung leading the Korean people even as he was being tortured.

He looked back at the past but what the leader said in the daytime rang in his ears.

"Now the workers are the masters of the works.... The workers and peasants who lived in rags and hunger in the past must build their country with their own hands.... We can do nothing without iron.... We must repair the works and produce iron as soon as possible.... For workers nothing in this world is impossible. We are looking forward to the day when iron is produced at the works...."

Every word reached his heart.

The words carried his deep faith in the poor workers and his great love for them, people who had been driven like cattle by the Japanese imperialists and the capitalists. Who on this earth had ever esteemed them so highly? Who on earth had ever loved or believed in them?

One after another, heartbreaking scenes of bitter past appeared before his eyes. His father was buried under a dam when he was working at a hydro-power station construction site. He started work at a Japanese iron works at 13 years of age and used to be struck heavily before he was driven away. Then he did hard toil at a steel works. Some of his friends fell into the oven of boiling iron from exhaustion from carrying ores. His eldest son died of pneumonia for lack of medicine. But General Kim Il Sung said that the workers and peasants who had been poverty-stricken in the past should become the masters of the country. For the General himself had said that, come what may, such a country would be built. The workers discussed the reconstruction of the works all night through in line with the General's instructions. We must found such a state without fail and uphold his teachings.

Ung Chil felt that his prospects became bright and that his heart was full of confidence, and new strength was growing up in his body.

"From now on I must live as taught by General Kim Il Sung, whole-heartedly supporting and believing in him. We must get that congealed iron out of the furnaces with chisels if we have to, for he told us to reconstruct the works and produce iron as soon as possible."

Ung Chil resolved firmly and his thoughts drifted to Byong Du.

"What is Byong Du doing now, while all the people here are in high spirits after meeting General Kim Il Sung? I'll bring him back! He'll be very glad to hear that the General visited the works."

Next day Ung Chil took the train to fetch Byong Du.

Everything was in disorder, for those were the first days after liberation. The train which started at noon arrived at XX station towards evening, but owing to some unavoidable circumstances the passengers were told to get off to take the train the next morning.

There was no other way for him.

Ung Chil got off and came out to the station front. It was a hell of a crowd!

Ung Chil came upon a sheet metal worker there who had left the works on the previous day. He learned from him that the Byong Dus were there waiting for the train.

Ung Chil was taken to a corner of the front of the station Byong Du's family were resting.

Byong Du noticing Ung Chil, ran out of the shade of an elm tree crying: "Isn't that you, Ung Chil? What wind has blown you here?"

"I've come to fetch you," Ung Chil said.

"To fetch me?"

"There's a particular reason. It's good luck that I've met you here!"

"Why?"

"Let's sit here first. I'll tell you in detail."

Meanwhile Byong Du's wife and children came running to him. Byong Du's youngest child clung to Ung Chil's sleeve.

As soon as they had sat down in the shade, Byong Du asked him, impatiently:

"What's the reason?"

"General Kim Il Sung visited our works," Ung Chil said, suppressing his excitement.

"General Kim Il Sung himself?" Byong Du's eyes sparkled.

"Brother! Is that true?" the sheet metal worker asked, quickly coming nearer.

"It is incredible?... Of course. Who would expect, of all things, that he would visit our works? But it is true."

"Well, did you really see him in person?" Byong Du was still incredulous.

"Of course I did. I talked to him, shook hands with him."

"He really shook your hand?"

"You can't believe it, can you?" Ung Chil said and he went on proudly, telling them all about it.

Byong Du and the sheet metal worker listened to him with bated breath.

Byong Du's wife wiped the corner of her eye with her coat ties.

"He said that we workers were the masters of the works and that leaving the works because our life was hard there would be resigning our right to be the masters.

"Byong Du! In the past neither you nor I were ever treated as human beings. We were despised by the whole world and made to live like animals. But the General looks on us as masters of the works and of the country How can we leave now when he is asking us to rebuild to produce iron as soon as possible? Byong Du, what do you think?"

Listening to him, Byong Du began to sob, his shoulders heaving. Byong Du's wife turned aside, hiding her face behind her skirt.

Byong Du raised his head and said, "Let's go back to the works, Ung Chil. Think of General Kim Il Sung! How can I go when General Kim Il Sung calls me? Let's go back right away and make the iron he is asking for."

"Brother I'll do the same," said the sheet metal worker.

The three went round the station and told other workers from the works of the news, and all of them decided to go back with them.

In fact the news spread ahead of them. Soon Ung Chil was surrounded by a crowd, and he could hardly keep up with their questions. There was a stir of excitement inside and outside the station.

As they would greet the sun after the long rains, the talk about General Kim Il Sung became animated. Ung Chil and the Byong Dus took the train back, whole-hearted in their determination to found the state under the wise leadership of General Kim Il Sung.

That was the beginning of the history of iron of liberated Korea.

How many were the bottlenecks and troubles that they met with before the great moment when finally, in General

Kim Il Sung's presence, they smelted the first iron after taking the solidified steel out of the dead furnaces piece by piece and bringing the furnaces back to life.

It was the first serious battle of the working class in power in building up the country's economy.

Ung Chil and Byong Du never went home till the day they lit the fire in the furnace.

They worked hard day and night.

While chiselling out the great lumps of steel in the furnace, they often wondered if they would ever succeed in finishing this heavy work. But Ung Chil would remember what the General had said:

The working class can do anything if they are resolved to do it.

That always encouraged him and made him more determined to produce the steel the General found so important.

Every time they met with difficulties, the workers remembered the General's words. They would hold a meeting and pool their strength and their ideas to overcome them.

Every word spoken by him was the source of strength that inspired them to glorious exploits.

Days passed, then weeks and months. And the workers showed no sign of fatigue in their battle.

Meanwhile, the situation at home and abroad changed.

The Party and people's power were founded and democratic reforms carried out: everything went just as the General had told Ung Chil. Workers and peasants' living conditions, too, improved thanks to the Party and Government he led.

One day Ung Chil and Byong Du were working at the furnace, when an official of the works who had been to Pyongyang came up to them, saying, "Comrade Ung Chil! General Kim Il Sung asked after your health. And he asked me to give you his regards."

"Why, does he still remember my name?" Ung Chil said in bewilderment.

"Not only your name but what you said when you met him," the official said. "I reported that you brought back Comrade Byong Du after you had met him and that you were working hard to rebuild the furnaces. He was well satisfied, and praised you as a true member of the working class."

"Why did you tell him? I havn't done anything much." The modest Ung Chil stuttered, blushing at General Kim Il Sung's praise.

"Well, I only told him the truth. He was anxious about your health. So you must take care of your health, however important your job may be. You mustn't worry him, must you?"

Ung Chil and Byong Du were very moved, and couldn't say a word. "Thank you very much, General!" they exclaimed to themselves.

The greater the General's favour, the more eager they were to get smelting as soon as possible both for the General's sake and for the country.

The great day came at last. That was the historic moment when the iron industry of free Korea was born. Working class iron that would make our country wealthy and strong, make the people's life happier and annihilate all aggressors.

The whole nation and the whole world were watching the great moment, and the enemy was full of anxiety and fear.

General Kim Il Sung walked slowly up to the red tape, with Ung Chil and Byong Du beside him. The General cut the tape with the scissors Ung Chil handed him. In a moment a cataract of yellowish red-hot molten iron gushed out of the furnace, with countless sparks flying about the air.

At once loud cheers and cries of "Long live General Kim Il Sung!" shook the whole place.

The General, smiling all over his face, gripped Ung Chil's and Byong Du's hands and said, "Now, let me grasp the hands of the heroes who have put life into the dead converter."

He went on, "Many thanks. Never ever has the iron congealed in a cold furnace been chiselled out lump by lump to get molten iron. Only our working class can do it."

So highly praised, Ung Chil and Byong Du could not restrain the hot tears that ran down their cheeks. "What's the matter—shedding tears on this happy day?" the General said smiling.

"General, we are so happy that..." Ung Chil could not finish the sentence.

"So am I, but we have many more furnaces that wait your

remarkable skill. We must continue our battle, drawing on the experience gained here."

The General again clasped Ung Chil's and Byong Du's hands.

"Give us any kind of work. We can do it," Ung Chil said confidently.

A few months later Ung Chil and Byong Du on orders of the General moved to this iron works to join in the reconstruction of furnace No. 1.

This was a harder task. Many problems cropped up on the way. The workers, however, overcame them one after another thinking of how molten iron would pour out before long.

As time went by Ung Chil grew to learn more clearly the great and deep meaning of the story of iron told by General Kim Il Sung when he met him for the first time.

There was a blizzard in the night, but the workers were busy working at the furnace. Ung Chil and young men were carrying in bricks that could be used to build furnace walls. The leader of building team ran up and told Ung Chil that the General wanted him on the telephone.

It was so unexpected that Ung Chil ran to the office as if in a trance. He picked up the receiver with a feeling of reverence.

"This is Pak Ung Chil speaking, General," Ung Chil said in a polite tone. The familiar voice rang through the phone:

"How are you, Comrade Ung Chil? I wanted to visit you there but I couldn't. I've been informed by your factory officials how things are going on there. How are you getting along? Is there any problem I could solve?"

"All requests we made the other day were granted thanks to your care. We have no more problems. Now things are going ahead as planned."

"How is your health? Are any of you ill?"

"We are all right, General."

"You must all take care of your health, it is cold these days."

"Thank you very much, General," Ung Chil said in a choked voice.

"Comrade Ung Chil!" the General went on talking. "Now the whole country is longing for the day when your rebuilt furnace produces iron. Can you do it by the date you set?"

"Yes, we can," Ung Chil said assuredly.

"Fine! Do it without fail. Your work has a great economic importance, too. Don't forget it."

"We won't forget it, General."

"And if you have any headache, don't hesitate to let me know. Remember me to your comrades," the General rang off.

The wall clock struck two.

Ung Chil saw the image of the General sitting up till late even in this night of snowstorm, looking after the nation's affairs and showing his concern for the health of the workers.

Ung Chil felt something pungent in his nostrils, and, for the sake of the General he was more than ever determined to give his all.

At last the workers brought the first molten iron out of furnace No. 1, too, in the presence of the General.

When the ceremony was over, the General took Ung Chil and Byong Du to the manager's office.

The General watched them carefully, and said: "You look very tired. I'm afraid you must take a rest."

"We are all right, General."

"No! Both your faces say, 'Honestly, we are quite worn out.' I can't sleep unless you are healthy, you know? Go to a rest home, a sanatorium or the seaside to rest till you have regained your health. If not, I will not be free from anxiety."

Ung Chil and Byong Du were so touched by his parental care that they couldn't utter a word and just stood silent, glued to the spot.

Thanks to the loyal working class ready to go through thick and thin when called upon by the leader, dead blast furnaces, open-hearth furnaces and rolling shops revived, and thus the history of our iron production was made. And it was not merely the history of iron.

It was a history of our liberated people's great struggle to found a strong, wealthy country for themselves, a history of our working class steeled and developed to full stature.

But, now, everything achieved with our people's blood and sweat was cruelly destroyed by the American imperialist aggressors....

Early this morning, while others were still in bed resting from fatigue, the leader visited the ruins of the iron works where you

could hardly move about and carefully inspected the terrible scars of the war Ung Chil was sure that the General was recalling bygone days, and a pang of sorrow shot through his heart.

However, Ung Chil yet felt invigorated, reassured, the moment he greeted the leader.

The leader is the national hero who for 20 years fought heavily armed Japanese imperialists and, despite all kinds of hardship, saved the country and the people from destruction. In those troublesome days after liberation, he founded people's power to give the workers factories, the peasants land and schools to the children. He revived factories and mills destroyed by Japanese imperialists, and turned this land to a flowering paradise, the envy of the world.

Didn't he inspire the whole nation to smash the American imperialists who had been so proud of being the "mightiest in the world", when they recklessly attacked us intending to swallow up this country? Aren't our country and our people called a heroic country and a heroic people because we are led by Marshal Kim Il Sung, the great leader of the whole Korean people?

Now, this morning only three days after the ceasefire, the great leader has visited the iron works that the enemy reduced to ruins. Ung Chil could not fully apprehend the great meaning of this fact. But he was thrilled to foresee the beginning of our people's new history which would be made under the great leader, which would astonish the world and strike terror into the hearts of enemies.

The leader passed the broken mess hall and came into the open-hearth furnace shop.

The deserted shop smelt of iron.

He scrutinized the damaged open-hearth furnaces for a long while, then turned his eyes to Ung Chil and with a meaningful smile said, "Comrade Ung Chil, the open-hearth furnaces are waiting for your hands."

"We are also anxious to produce iron as early as possible, but, honestly, we don't know where to begin," Ung Chil said with a puzzled look.

"I understand just how you feel. But you have begun the work already."

Ung Chil was perplexed at these unexpected words.

"We haven't done anything, General."

"You have. You were doing it this morning," the General said and smiled.

Ung Chil couldn't understand what he had done.

The General, still smiling, went on, "Comrade Ung Chil, the knapsack you are carrying tells it. The reconstruction of the works should be begun by picking up the nuts and bolts as you are doing. It may seem like a trifle, but what a noble spirit dwells in it! It shows you workers how patriotically we can serve the country by rebuilding foundries and producing iron quickly and manifest your hatred for the enemy."

The leader stopped talking for a while and then he added:

"When the Japanese imperialists surrendered, they destroyed the furnaces without removing the molten iron. They scarpered, and they claimed that the Koreans wouldn't be able to rebuild the furnaces. But, burning with patriotism and hatred for the Japs, you workers removed the lumps of iron with chisels and were smelting iron in a little over a year, weren't you? Now the Americans are telling the same kind of story. And you are already preparing to put their noses out of joint as you did in the war. If they knew this, they would tremble like leaves." The leader laughed aloud.

Now Ung Chil understood the full importance of what he was doing.

Getting out of the open-hearth furnace shop the leader walked slowly up a weedy hillock within the works compound.

Ung Chil followed him and he was deeply sorry for he was walking through grass wet with dew. How often has the leader cut his way through untrodden roads to lead his people at the first grey of dawn!

Ung Chil was moved to tears. Walking up the slope the leader advised that they should rebuild the open-hearth furnaces first but, instead of trying to get on with all of them at once, they would do better to do them one by one, consulting with each other and taking their capacity, materials and equipment into account.

Ung Chil engraved every word of the great leader Marshal

~~Kim Il Sung~~ in his mind so that it was clear to him what was to be done from now on. And he felt new strength and courage welling up within him; he was confident that they could rebuild the works by their own efforts.

Soon they were on the top of the hillock. From there they could see that the whole wide compound was now clear of fog.

The eastern sky was glowing red, announcing sunrise. New leaves and twigs on the acacias scorched and broken by the enemy's bombs were rustling in the breeze. Birds were chirping. The leader looked tenderly at the trees.

Ung Chil recalled the day the leader visited his works years before, when he said few factories had so many trees in the compounds and advised them to look after them.

Pointing at the trees the leader said, "Just look at them, Comrade Ung Chil. They were bombed, too, and broken, cut and scorched. But they survived and have so many boughs and twigs now. That is because American bombs could not damage their roots in the ground. Isn't that so, Comrade Ung Chil?"

"It is, dear leader!"

"The Yanks used every possible means to force us to give in, but they couldn't touch our roots, the roots fed on the noble blood of the anti-Japanese guerrillas. In the last war, too, a lot of heroes faithful to the Party like Byong Du defended the roots at the cost of their lives. As long as the roots are kept alive, they are certain to put forth buds and twigs and bear fruit. No force on earth can hit our revolutionary roots."

After a few moments he resumed: "Comrade Ung Chil, we need iron more badly than ever before. We are going to give heavy industry priority while working simultaneously on light industry and agriculture. Only then can we recover from our war wounds and build up our economic foundations to make the country wealthy and strong. Then we can quickly improve the people's living conditions and strengthen national defences in order to smash the American imperialists if they attack again. This is the only road for us to take.

"Of course it is a thorny road. But we can do it. We are the Koreans who defeated the Americans. We have the heroic working class and the basis of heavy industry. Even in the difficult days of the war the Party, looking ahead into the future, built large machine factories that will guarantee the priority development of heavy industry, and we have trained technicians, too. If we make good use of them, we can tackle any task.

"We must build even bigger open-hearth furnaces on the ruins of the old ones that the Americans have broken and brick buildings where before there were thatched houses, and show them the mettle of the Korean people. Comrade Ung Chil, do you think you can do it?"

"I do, dear leader. There is nothing impossible as long as we are with you," Ung Chil answered in a trembling voice, hugely excited.

"No, Comrade Ung Chil" the leader said. "You are the source of our strength. Whenever I face hardship, I think of you comrades. I can see already the magnificent foundry that you will build".

Slowly the leader, full of dignity and confidence, ran his eyes over the whole compound.

Before Ung Chil's eyes, too, there appeared a panoramic view of the great metallurgy centre that soon would rise from debris under the leader's great plan.

Rows of furnaces, giving off black clouds of smoke; open-hearth furnaces filled with boiling iron; rivers of molten iron gushing out, red and yellow sparks flying about like confetti; giant coke ovens built on the riverside; huge rolling shops with modern equipment; rails all over the compound with busy waggons moving up and down loaded with mountains of cauldrons, steel ingots and plates; multi-storeyed buildings, windows glittering in the sun and an iron city covered with rustling green trees; happy inhabitants enjoying their lives; guns and tanks on the impregnable front line reliably defending them all....

Ung Chil could hardly suppress his excitement. He was happy to have the great and wise leader Comrade Kim Il Sung and was proud of being one of his soldiers.

We will carry out the new task you've assigned us without fail, Ung Chil pledged to himself.

Our history of iron which began under the guidance of the great leader will continue under his command, startling the world with many miracles.

1967

Happiness

Sok Yun Gi

Sin Hyong Jin, the famous surgeon, was in my class in middle school and a childhood friend.

Now we are over forty, but we have remained close friends all these years. Our long friendship is above all based on the fact that we have a similar turn of mind. But there is more to it than that. Our backgrounds are rather similar too. He was a poor farmer's son and mine was a poor teacher's family. We both worked our way through school in early life. But after our country's liberation thanks to the Party's solicitude, we finished university, and both entered professions.

He taught at a university of medicine. Later he was a medical officer at a field hospital and now he is a surgeon in hospital. His chosen field was medicine, mine journalism.

Different professions, of course, made our personal contacts less frequent. But still it was nice when we were both in Pyongyang. My house was always open to him. He used to come over on Sundays or sometimes drop in in the late evening for a chat. Even later when he moved away from Pyongyang he used to stay with us for several days whenever his work brought him to the city.

He is what you call hefty, six feet and good at sports right from his school years. He sang folk songs rather well in a deep, resonant voice and he occasionally appeared on the stage with other music group members. Often I wondered if he had chosen the right profession—after all, surgery requires precision, a quality that I somehow do not associate with him.

But there he is an authority in his chosen field. Particularly, during the last few years he has successfully operated on over 500 patients—people who maimed and crippled, had been regarded as incurable. His name is known in every corner of the land. I sometimes think his huge frame and powerful voice became useful assets in making his name.

He was persuaded by his seniors and research centres to prepare a thesis for a doctorate—after all he has had many years of clinical experience. He presented his thesis a little while ago and is in Pyongyang now to defend it.

He rang me at the office. So, as soon as I got home I asked my wife, who was busy in the kitchen:

"Isn't Hyong Jin here yet?"

"No! Is he in town?" she asked, wide-eyed.

"He arrived early this morning. I thought he would be home by now to have supper with us. He rang me up. Maybe something is delaying him." I murmured, in no mood to eat my supper.

"What shall I do then? We should cook something special for him...."

"Why something special? He is one of us!"

"But as he hasn't been here for a long time, then won't he blame us for the poor supper?"

She took no notice of what I had said. I could see her making up her mind. She cleared the table, evidently to prepare another supper!

Some time later Hyong Jin appeared with a fair-sized suitcase. By then his meal was almost ready. It was our first meeting after the Party Congress of the previous year, but he walked in without ceremony. Not that he ever was a stickler for punctilio.

First he went into the children's bedroom (the children were in bed by then) to leave sweets and toys he had brought, then he came into my room. He was less interested in the grown-ups, but always knew what the children needed and never failed to bring them presents. My wife teased him as she was setting the table:

"Doctor! You always remember the children, but never me! You know, you never find a wife that way!"

Hyong Jin glanced at me and burst out laughing.

When supper was over, I invited him to take a walk along the Taedong River.

This was the first time we had gone for a walk and chat after a long separation. We used to do it when we were in school, talking about the revolution and our dreams.... There were heated discussions at times. As we grew up, somehow our strolls became fewer. This river is very dear to us because our young dreams blossomed there. So we were always sad to think we were drifting away from this riverside, the place of our young dreams.

That night the moon was serene. Its mellow light streamed through the early spring mist that spread like a sticky liquor across the calm river. The dark water gently rippled. It was high tide and the swelling water seemed to be trying to jump over the riverside path as if it had something to tell us. One by one it climbed the steps. The Okryu Bridge lights in the water looked like giant candlesticks. Perhaps if one went down riding the rainbow bridge of candlesticks, one might get to the legendary crystal palace. The bright scene in the water was indeed a fairyland.

The hour was late, and only a few shadowy figures could be seen on the broad walks.

We walked on, saying little.

"No prospect this year either?"

"I don't know!"

I broke the silence with a question but his answer was less than enthusiastic.

As I have said, he is quite a carefree person. But as soon as the word remarriage is mentioned and I do that every time I see him, he freezes up.

I still remember the time when he finished university after liberation and came back to teach at his old school after spending a few years at a research institute. He was still boyish, a jolly fellow, much more so, when he married. To me his happy marriage almost made him seen like an innocent boy again.

It was around this time that I introduced him and his wife to my wife. We two couples used to go on outings together—five of us (we had a baby then named Yun). We used to go for a picnic on Yanggak or Rungna Island in the Taedong River which we could not discern now in the darkness. But I felt I could almost hear Hyong Jin singing a folk song Yangsando in his admirable bass, which he used to do on those occasions.

But during the war while he was serving in a field hospital his wife and Ok Hui—that was their little girl's name—were killed in a barbarous enemy air raid.

I was a front-line correspondent. It was with sorrow that I learned of this tragic event when my paper had sent for me to Pyongyang. But it was sadder still to have to tell him the bad news in detail afterwards when I met him. I felt my heart was torn to pieces as I broke the news!

We were surprised when he was demobbed and came to see us after the truce. He walked in just as if nothing had happened.

Of course, I knew there was a sorrow deep in his heart. He tried to hide it, and my heart ached. He could not express himself in these matters. But we had known all along that he had loved his wife and baby very dearly.

So, you cannot blame me if I wanted to see him happy again. As a matter of fact, for the last few years, I have been trying to coax him to marry again. Of course, I could not bring up the subject before I was sure that the wounds in his heart healed up. This is something one has to go slow about. For one thing, whenever I bring up the question, he cuts me short. And I have not got very far on the subject.

A few years ago I was in his county. I saw him at his hospital, where someone told me he was getting serious about a woman, an assistant doctor. I was pleased to hear this. But he never told me what became of it.

We kept walking, each busy with his own thoughts, and we passed the Taedong Gate. I wanted to try again. In a rather grumbling tone I shot questions at him.

"Well, how about it? I think it's about time you began to think about your own happiness. How long do you intend to go on like this?"

But he did not open his mouth. His eyes were fixed on the water breaking against the bank sending back racing ripples.

"As you know, our papers keep writing about you. We say you have made a great contribution to the people's happiness. You certainly have, and the government has honoured you. But let me ask you, how about you, yourself? Now, in this era everyone has a happy life. But where is your happiness? Where?"

He seemed to be determined to say nothing on this topic, no matter how hard I tried.

Whenever a bus crossed the Taedong Bridge the whole river used to reverberate with the rumble. You could see golden images trembling on the water. Leaning against a lamp-post he gazed at the Revolution Museum and the roof of the Grand Theatre. Then he turned his eyes across the river, from where the humming of some machines could be heard, and now and then a welder's torch lit up the sky. Suddenly he asked, jocularly:

"Tell me, Chol. Are you a happy man?"

"Me?"

He had caught me off my guard. That was the question I had last expected. When I spoke of his happiness, of course I had taken it for granted that I was happy. But now this question, point-blank!

In all modesty, I can say that I am doing my share for the Party and the revolution, I would not say I am the best in my line but neither am I the worst. Then I have a nice home. There is my wife, I don't know many women better. And the three children! The boy is doing very well at school, and the two girls are darlings. And they are all healthy. Of course I sometimes wish my parents were alive to see all this but that's all. Is there anything that I should feel bad about? I am happy, aren't I? While all this passed through my mind Hyong Jin went on:

"There you are! You cannot answer my question. So, I suspect that you are not quite as happy as you thought. Right?"

I tried to stop him, but he laughed. Soon he was serious again.

"Of course, I was joking! I dare say you're the happiest of men. But I am sure you haven't given too much thought to what happiness is."

I could not agree entirely, and I kept silent as he sounded more serious than ever.

"Happiness... you think I am unhappy, don't you? That's why you so often talk about happiness ironically whenever you see me. But I wonder if you've not degenerated in a way. What is happiness? You tell me."

I mumbled something. I must admit, the way he presented things was so extraordinary that my answer was hardly to the point. And he knew it. He even sneered at what I had said. He lit a cigarette. He seemed to be trying to shake off the unpleasant note he evidently had felt in my answer. After a puff or two he poured out:

"What you are saying is simply vulgar. A beautiful wife.... Of course, I would like that. But like youth, beauty is gone all too soon. Then what will happen to your happiness? A wife getting on in years! Serving the Party and revolution, the pride you take in your work, adorable children, a rich life—it seems you have made quite a list of lusts. But do you think happiness is as complicated as that? In this country from olden times there has been the saying that one needs Five Blessings to be a happy man. So how many blessings do you have? Suppose you are a woman. Then you would also include the number of dresses you have among your blessings, wouldn't you?"

I was furious. As in our younger days, we had got into a heated argument. But this time I had got into the defensive from the outset. Hyong Jin had the initiative and, now and then, he even compromised to stop me feeling too bad. I was getting all heated. I felt that if I lost in the argument, the whole thing would backfire and my dear friend would suffer. But Hyong Jin was calm as ever.

"Well, Chol! I feel that too often we look at happiness from outside, not realizing what is at the core. To a sensualist happiness may lie in a beautiful woman; to a Shylock money is the whole world. You don't give a hoot for your health because you're healthy. But to the sick nothing is more precious than health. To me it seems that all this is not happiness but an illusion. Some people think that if they get all they are after they are happy. But I think man is naturally great enough not to see such satisfactions as happiness. The more so we who are communists, the noblest of men. So it is as true communists that we must seek our happiness. Don't misunderstand me. I'm no puritan. I've no objection to a beautiful wife. I know that one must gratify one's desire up to a point and build a happy home."

"Well, if that is what you think, why can't you put it into practice? That's what surprises me. I don't know if you realize it or not, but you are like a Buddha!" I was getting all hot under the collar and was on the attack.

"I know you mean that I should marry. But it is something that doesn't necessarily go as I might wish. All right, as you say I am a Buddha. But Buddha cannot shave his own head!"

At this point, our argument made a sudden turn, of which I was glad. Then I asked him in a more relaxed manner:

"Tell me this. I heard some time ago you were taking an interest in an assistant doctor. What happened to her?"

For a moment he looked puzzled. He glanced at me and murmured, and a little smile played on his lips.

"I take my hat off to you newspapermen. How on earth did you know about that?"

"You're right. After all, I am a newspaperman. But tell me first what became of her?"

"She got married."

"Married? They said you went around with her—a lie, eh?"

"Yeah! It's true I did, and in a way I loved her, I suppose."

"Then what happened?"

"Oh, I don't know. And you might well think, too, that it could have been partly my fault."

A breeze had sprung up, and the river began to rage, wetting our spring overcoats with a fine spray. Countless stars were reflected in the water, crushed by the ripples, the mirrors strewn all over the dark surface of the water.

We turned around, our pace as leisurely as ever.

I tried to make out what Hyong Jin could have meant when he said "it could have been partly his own fault". Maybe, my friend was also turning things over in his mind. His eyes fixed on the dark river, he just kept walking. Suddenly he broke the silence.

"Chol, of course you know what I mean. I believe that we can say we are happy when we hear our own steps in the great movement of the people towards progress and in their fighting ranks. When we see ourselves in the great Chollima march headed by the great leader, helping others and being led by others in this vigorous advance of the revolution, that, to me, is happiness. What I am saying is this—true happiness is to be found when the happiness of individuals and that of society fuse completely into one, say, the happiness provided by our Party. In that sense, I cannot say I have happiness. But there are times I am intoxicated with a sense of happiness."

This sounded like some sort of a confession. Yet I had to concede one point. I was the loser of the argument.

In the dim light I found something noble in his muscular face, something that I had not noticed all these forty years. There were, to be sure, a few lines on his face, and his temples were beginning to grey. (I told myself I was right. He should get cracking and get married.) But I could read in his suntanned face sincerity, enthusiasm, optimism—the very features of our era.

"I expect you want to hear about what happened between the assistant doctor and me, don't you?" I felt his truthful tone and nodded. He went to a bench and said, grinning, "I know you'll come back to this unless I tell you all about it.... But I am warning you. Leave your newspaper out of it—not that it is worth printing."

His words recalled his wife to my memory. Now I hoped—though I had no way of knowing how the story would turn out—no shadow would darken his heart again. Quietly I sat down beside him.

For some time he sat staring across the river at the clouds

gathering in the sky. Eventually he began the story.

Told in the first person, it ran something like this:

Early one morning in late July in 1955 I got off the train at V station.

You may recall there were people who said that I chose that particular place because I wanted to find a sanctuary in which to nurse my pain and heartache over my lost family. People could not understand why I stopped teaching at the college.

From the army I had gone to the university. As a matter of fact, I was still in uniform only without epaulettes. But have you ever thought about who my students were? I had to lecture to much-decorated veterans. I must confess I really did not know how to go about it. I lectured on the theory of a renowned academician. Admirable as it was, it was not enough for these honest people who had shed blood for the country; many of them had been wounded, had seen their comrades die.

Of course I too had been in the war. But where had I been? In a field hospital way behind the lines. In the operating theatre. Of course, my three years at the front taught me a lot. An ordinary man, a surgeon, I grew into a Party member and a revolutionary fighter, though there was much still to be desired in me.

And I returned asking a then unanswerable question. I realized that to the heroic people of this land the word "man" meant more than a biological entity of cell tissues and different systems. As I said, the war years had taught me a lot, yet they presented many questions. For instance, I asked myself, do I, as a surgeon, have the right to let death take these people away? If not, what am I supposed to do? Which is more important in treatment, modern medicine or human will?

As an instructor I should be able to answer when students ask such questions and I was unprepared. So, one might say that my going to the town of V—where the patients were, especially many disabled soldiers—was in a way running away from the dignity and rigidity of science.

Then I must mention another point. After all, I'm in no way unusual. It would be untrue if I said that I never think of my dead wife and child. But whether you believe this or not, something more powerful even than grief took over. A thirst for revenge. That's right. I wanted to revenge myself upon the enemy who had taken my comrades and my loved ones. The cursed Yankees—I must have revenge, a hundred-fold, a thousand-fold.

The night journey had rather taken it out of me, but my heart was light as I made my way to the county hospital in that strange place.

It was still dark, I remember. The town was then in the throes of rebuilding. A few new brick buildings stood here and there around the railway station and along the central thoroughfare. But between these buildings there were many vacant lots which had been cleared of rubble. Only the old concrete foundations could be seen in the grey early light. And the rows of young, newly planted trees waved their branches in the morning breeze as if to greet me. And I felt so "close" to the young trees because, after all, like them, I was a sapling transplanted into strange soil.

As I walked in the grey twilight I kept thinking: what kind of soil is this I'm in? I wanted to meet people as quickly as possible. I speeded up my pace to the hospital. The county hospital was not in the town but on a hill some way off. I found out that the building had been the office of an experimental farm.

When I arrived there, I was early and found no outpatients of course. The whole place was quiet. I went around from one room to another, but not a soul was to be seen.

I opened the door of the treatment room expecting to find a doctor on duty. But this was empty too. It was spick and span, and had obviously just been cleaned. And the air was clean and tinged with that special hospital smell. For a moment I wondered where everybody was.

Suddenly a woman's shrill laughter broke the silence. It came from the back yard, so I ran out. The yard rose gradually toward the mountain. An old zelkova tree stood there and a woman in a white gown, knelt on the ground and kept saying:

"Come on out, you little devil! Come out, do you hear me?"

What on earth? I stood there open-mouthed. Judging from the voice, she was a young woman. So I could hardly just barge in. She stayed there, threatening one minute and laughing the next.

Feeling awkward, I stood still and watched. But I could not just go on standing there indefinitely.

So I moved slowly towards the big tree near where she was.

Evidently she had an animal cage under the tree for experiments. It seemed she was playing with an animal and it was hiding itself behind a rock beside the cage. The girl laughed, coaxed, threatened. When the animal did not come out she scolded it. Now it looked hopeless and I thought she was near to tears.

"Don't make me cross by hiding there. Come out at once. Do you hear me?"

The rock was not a big one. I stepped forward determinedly.

"Excuse me, but has something run away?"

She started and jumped to her feet.

It was not yet completely light, but I could see her, a vigorous girl with a radiant face. Her presence seemed to fill the air with sweetness. Something in her laughter had a familiar ring creating a cordial atmosphere. To my question, she answered most apologetically:

"It is a white mouse. It was so cute that I took it out while I was feeding it. Now it's gone and hid."

She was so upset about it that she had no time to give me, a total stranger, another thought. She was as innocent as a child.

"Are you sure it went back behind the rock?" I asked. "It might have run away to the mountain."

"Oh, it couldn't! It is docile, it couldn't run," she answered, trying to defend the white mouse.

"Then, let it stay there."

"No, it is intended for experiments...."

I wanted to tease her and her tearful tone. But I could not very well do so.

Telling her that if she had to have it back I would help her, I shifted the rock. Sure enough there was a white mouse digging into the soft soil, rolling its pink eyes. It did not even try to run away. Really it looked so cute, even I could not help smiling.

"You naughty little thing!"

She was so glad to find it, she let out a cry of joy and snatched it up in a flash. She stroked a few times before putting it back in the cage.

Now, becoming conscious of my presence, she looked me over from head to toe

"Thank you so much By the way, have you come so early to see a doctor?"

"No, I'm the new head of the surgical department."

"Oh!"

She stared.

"Then you must be Dr. Sin Hyong Jin.... I'm so sorry. I am Li Ok Ju, I work in your department."

She seemed glad to see me. The hospital director had been notified of my coming from the provincial seat so everyone was expecting me. And I felt flattered to learn that they had been waiting for me, thinking that I could be of some service to them. But at the same time a new sense of the weight of my responsibility bore down my assurance. But I must say also that it does not make you feel so bad starting a new life knowing everyone around you is expecting something of you. And I was delighted to have a cheerful, innocent assistant like Ok Ju. A personality like her can brighten the surgery—sometimes it can be gloomy.

She led me to the "treatment" room. It was getting lighter outside, but I had still not had a chance to have a good look at her. Now she carried the bunch of flowers she had left on the cage and a small pail containing her toiletries.

In the hospital corridor I noticed that she wore a white flower in the back of her hair. Evidently, when she was out to wash her face in the yard after cleaning the room, she had picked flowers for the patient, before she had the trouble with the white mouse.

I tell you frankly I felt good about things, I felt serene. She carried a fragrance about her which cleared away all the fatigue of the overnight train journey as if it had worked wonders in my head. I was as calm as could be.

When I walked into the room, she turned round and smiled. For the first time in the bright light I had a chance to see her face—a beautiful, vivacious face. I stood there transfixed, staring at her.

Why? Because I saw Kyong Suk in her! Remember Kyong Suk who you told me was dead and where she was buried! I

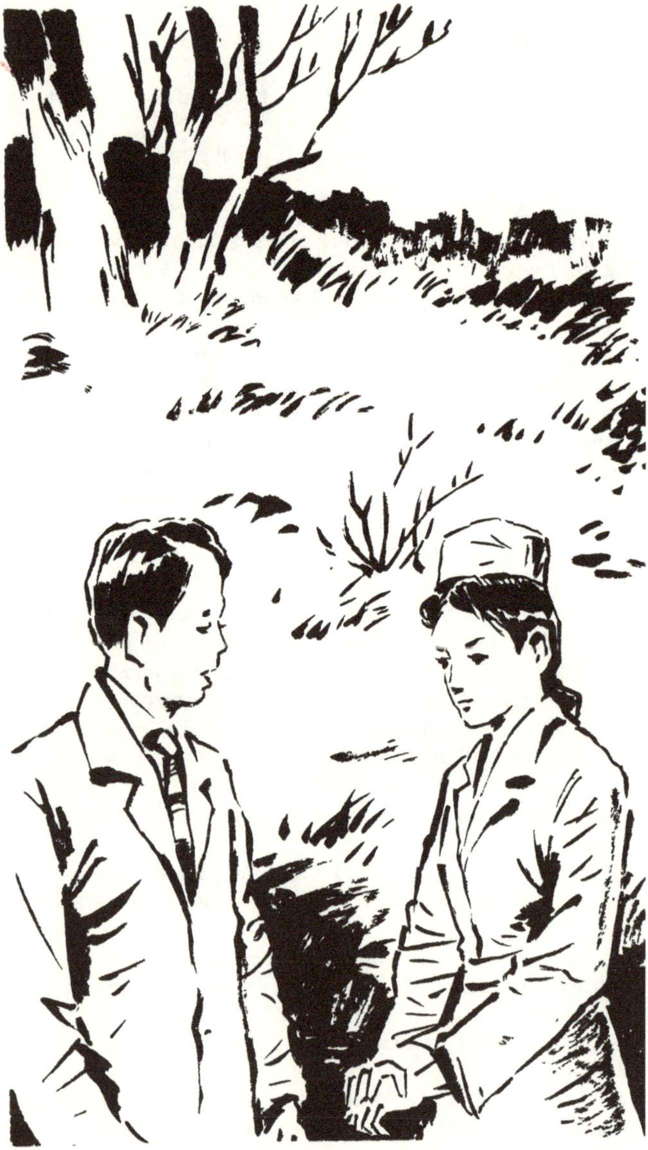

can speak of it now. But at that moment it flashed across my mind that you had played a nasty trick on me!

Here my friend paused The river began to stir. It was darker now, and the early spring air was chilly. Our spring overcoats flapped in the wind and a lock of his long hair blew across his high forehead.

I gathered that Ok Ju was the assistant doctor whom I had heard about.

Hyong Jin's wife had been beautiful, though if you asked me which of her features made her so, I would not know. But she was a beautiful woman with dark, deep-set eyes, a slightly pointed nose, full lips, and soft hair falling to her shoulders. Then there was the way she carried herself, her graceful figure. Her forehead on its own might have been trifle high perhaps, and a slight minus. But on her face even the minus became a plus.

My friend Hyong Jin used to stroll along this promenade with his wife. Remembering all this, I could easily imagine what he had experienced when he got to the new hospital. It must have been quite a shock for him.

Hyong Jin lit a cigarette. After a few puffs, he continued with his story in a calm voice.

The shock left me in a state of confusion. Perhaps you can imagine that I looked pale. Looking at me she asked, surprised:

"Doctor! Is something wrong? Are you ill?"

I pulled myself together, not to make a fool of myself in front of her, and spoke, though with a slight tremor in my voice:

"No! Nothing is wrong. It is just a bit stuffy in here. I'm going out to the waiting room."

To tell you the truth, the room was pleasant. The air was fresh and cool in the early morning breeze. I was afraid she had noticed my embarrassment. I rushed out to the waiting room as if running away. She watched me go. I could sense her question and a shadow of—even I could call it a shadow of sadness in her round eyes.

That was our first quite extraordinary meeting. And this

curious sense of frustration carried over into our work

I was head of the surgical department and she was an assistant doctor working under me. The funny thing was that I found myself avoiding. The first unhappy meeting was always in my mind and I simply could not shake it off.

Gradually I learned that Ok Ju was 23 and single. But with the very poor figure I cut in her presence at our first meeting, she seemed afraid of me, so she too avoided me.

As I said, she was cheerful. Songs and laughter followed her everywhere. If she went into a ward of very sick people, they ceased to groan. But if I entered it all changed. That I could sense. I was a bit of a wet blanket, which is not a nice thing to be.

In this way, though probably not intentional, there was a great divide between us.

Myself, I tried to be matter-of-fact and businesslike with her. By now she seemed to me to be much too friendly to everybody, frivolous almost. I began to think she was not what I had believed her to be.

Don't ask me what drove me, because I didn't know myself. At any rate, time flew by, and I just seemed to let things pass me by—the things that I as head of the department should have attended to.

Meanwhile I concentrated on my research. In a sense, it was my way of forgetting everyday things.

As you know, during the war I had chosen several research subjects in osteotomy. My going to the town of V itself had had something to do with that work. I wanted to complete it there. Whenever I had the chance I visited disabled soldiers or had them come to the hospital for observation. My days were full.

Soon the country was to celebrate the 10th anniversary of August 15 liberation.

At my hospital there was to be a circle performance under the auspices of the Democratic Youth League to entertain the patients. The preparations had got under way before I got there. I don't know how they learned that I could sing, but they insisted on my doing a turn. I tried to dodge it, but I failed. I was about 35 then so I was more ready to make a fool of myself. So though there was little chance of a rehearsal I promised then a solo and to sing in the chorus.

The celebrations were held on the evening of the 14th The patients were wheeled into the club room, where the whole staff and their families also assembled So you can imagine how crowded the place was. And I'll tell you, no professional theatre in the capital ever had such an enthusiastic audience There was an air of family intimacy mixed with good-natured bantering and joking typical of such gatherings.

Not only the patients but everyone was in a gay mood on the eve of the holiday.

That night Ok Ju was lovelier than ever. She was dressed in white, which suited her, and she looked both healthy and dignified.

On the backdrop there were hung a portait of our great leader and the flags of the Republic. Flowers and coloured ribbons decorated the stage When Ok Ju appeared on the stage the audience went wild. I'm sure that few artists ever had such a reception. It was genuine applause, straight from the heart. People were expressing their gratitude, and they were also proud of her as one of them.

How she sang that night! I had not thought that she could sing like that, all I had heard her do was hum. But the way she sang! Her voice was beautiful and she knew how to use it. And she sang in a clear tone, with such enthusiasm and appeal, she was as good as any professional that night.

As she sang the audience sat enraptured.

My turn was after Ok Ju, so I was backstage while she sang her number. I noticed an elderly woman waiting for her by the stage door. The woman caught Ok Ju by the hand as she came off stage and took her to a corner They were alike to look at (I later learned that she was her mother) It seemed she had something rather urgent to tell Ok Ju, and she spoke in a whisper, gesticulating a great deal. Of course, I had no idea of what she was saying but I noticed a shadow flitted across Ok Ju's face as she listened.

Meanwhile the audience went on applauding. They wanted Ok Ju back, shouting encore.

She seemed upset, but presently she ran back on to the stage. Even to my ears her encore was not as good. She was far from sure of herself, and her voice faltered. But it was good enough for the audience. Again there was a burst of applause.

I could tell how much the patients and the hospital staff loved her. It made me wonder why my impressions of her had been so different.

But this time, as soon as she descended from the stage, she rushed to the Democratic Youth League chairman to exchange a few words.

Then she looked around. Maybe she was looking for me. As I was about to step on the stage, she rushed to the pharmacy. Soon both of them—Ok Ju and her mother—disappeared.

The clapping did not abate. The master of ceremonies tried everything to quiet the audience, but they would not have "No" for an answer. They kept calling Ok Ju. And the master of ceremonies, head of the pharmaceutical department, was at a loss; he waited a moment, not knowing what to do. It put me in a very awkward position, for I was ready in the wings. I did not know whether to go on or to return to my seat.

What were we to do with the shouting people? Were they a regular theatre crowd? No, not a bit of it: they were the patients to whom we were ready to give everything—blood and flesh, if necessary.

But where was Ok Ju? She was to sing in the chorus, too, but she had gone. I said to myself. She must have had a good reason but, after all, it was personal. The whole thing left a feeling of unpleasantness with me.

The master of ceremonies, sweating profusely, went back to the stage to calm the audience. After much appealing, he managed to go on with the programme.

Her demeanour hurt my feelings. I thought, after all she sang well everywhere and at any time, then why all of a sudden when the people most wanted her to sing....

A few days later I received a notification that my Party transfer papers had arrived.

I went to the county Party office. There were quite a number of people waiting in the ante-room to the Party Membership Card Department, and I was among them. It was stuffy and I went outside. Whenever I went to a Party office I saw many I could learn from. That day was no exception. There were statistical personnel carrying their files, and departmental instructors; and Party members who came to discuss personal matters. Even the pretty rose mosses and zinnias in the garden had a meaningful look about them.

I looked at the wall slogan It read:

We should consolidate politically, economically and militarily the democratic base in the northern half of the Republic, which is the firm guarantee for the reunification and independence of the country. To this end, we should carry out the Three-Year Plan for the Postwar Rehabilitation and Development of the National Economy successfully.

Kim Il Sung

I remembered it was an excerpt of the great leader's closing speech at the Party Central Committee's April Plenary Meeting. Suddenly a voice behind me said: "Look! Isn't that Comrade Sin Hyong Jin?"

It was the county Party chairman who was returning from some business. I had met him only briefly when I went to report my arrival. As I said, it had been a brief encounter; he had to go to a meeting. Yet he remembered my name and called me like an old friend.

I learned that he had been a good scaffold worker in the days of Japanese oppression. Apparently there was not a construction site where he had not worked. Now, greying at the temples, he is an impressive looking man, very sociable, a man who likes a joke.

"How are you, Comrade Chairman?"

He shook hands warmly with me, with a broad smile.

"Fine, thanks. Otherwise, I would have come to see you, doctor. So, what brings you here?"

I told him I was there to take my transfer papers, but the Party chairman—evidently thinking of something else, unexpectedly shot a question at me in a somewhat serious tone.

"I hear Comrade Sung Jae was very ill on the holiday. Is it true?" I had not the slightest idea of what he was talking about. In the first place, who was this Sung Jae? I had never heard of him. For a moment, I thought he meant one of my patients, and was rebuking me for something that I had done or neglected to do. One by one, I ran over all the patients in my mind. There was none by that name. Besides, there had been no serious case on the holiday, inpatients or out. Yet, I knew that the Party chairman was not a person who would joke about a thing like that.

I was perplexed and did not know how to answer. So I was relieved when the registration window called out my name. Like a person saved from some great calamity, I answered in a loud voice.

"Here I am!"

The county Party chairman knew that I should not be detained and he started to walk away.

"Well, they are calling you. But please come to my office when you're through. I wanted to see you anyway," he called back.

I did not feel quite at ease when I knocked on his door. I had a nagging feeling that I had done something wrong. No matter how hard I tried, I could not remember any person called Sung Jae. Perhaps he was talking about someone who had been ill there before I came, I thought. Or he had got the name wrong though that seemed unlikely. The Party chairman did not make that kind of mistake.

I found the chairman talking to a propaganda department instructor. They were discussing how best to explain the report of the great leader delivered at the meeting celebrating the 10th anniversary of August 15 liberation to Party members. Presently their conversation ended and the chairman told him:

"Please bring over the radio. I mean Comrade Sung Jae's. Perhaps we can ask the doctor here to take it to him."

It seemed things were getting more complicated. When the man left the room, the chairman turned to me asking about my work and everything.

He wanted to know if I was feeling at home in the hostel, and if my research was coming along all right. When I told him I was quite all right, he gave a dubious, faint smile.

"I think I understand why you speak that way. No one is very happy when he has lost his loved ones. But we cannot afford to go on grieving. Perhaps you should have a home of your own again. Of course, that is up to you, but I rather think it would be better for you and also for your work. When that happens... Well, tell me about your research programmes.

How are they coming along?"

I told him everything that I was doing, not that it was that much. Moreover, there was nothing that I could tell him in concrete terms, nothing beyond rather general plans. I wanted his advice. But, listening to me, he became quite excited.

"Well, that sounds good. Of course, I know very little about those things, but I can say this much—it seems what you are doing is one that Party scientists should tackle and bring to fruition. The American devils crushed many of our young men's bones. And many cases have been pronounced incurable.

"You know what people used to say. A hunchback will remain a hunchback even in the next world. But if you can do something for them, it would be simply wonderful. I must say, it will be a slap in the face of the Yankees, also a slap on such proverbial sayings. I bet the old saying speaks of pains and sufferings the people had to endure. Sung Jae is in the same boat, too. According to what you're saying it means even he might be cured. Right? How wonderful that would be!"

As the chairman's voice became more agitated, I became more uneasy. It is true I had started my studies because my thoughts ran along that line. But how clear and simple the chairman's words were. Me? All my ideas were vague, surrounded in mist, and not on such a grand scale. Then, he linked his words with a person called Sung Jae. I felt awkward. I don't know if he read my thoughts but the question popped up again:

"Well, how is Sung Jae, by the way? Is he any better?"

"I'm sorry but I don't think I know exactly whom you are talking about. You don't mean Kim Sung Su in ward No. 8?"

At my mumbling, he frowned.

"Kim Sung Su? I mean Sung Jae, Comrade Ok Ju's husband!"

"What? Ok Ju's husband? I thought...."

Well, if ever there was a thunderbolt out of the blue sky, that was it. I just stood there dumbfounded like a person who had been hit over the head. What did he mean by the husband of a single girl?

The county Party chairman could not believe his ears when I confessed my ignorance of this person. He just fixed his eyes on me for some minutes before turning away. He seemed greatly displeased. I did not know what to do with myself; I was sitting on pins and needles. The worst part of it was that I did not know what I had bungled; what blunder had I made.

I sat there with my head hung in shame. The voice of the chairman came again. I could sense he was not in a jovial mood, and certainly not joking. He spoke in a serious tone. Sometimes his voice was filled with pain, sometimes heavy and severe.

"So in the last analysis you know nothing about him. I'm really sorry to hear it. I expect that is my own fault. After all, you have only been here three weeks or so, and that around a holiday. So, I suppose it is quite possible for you not to know all this. Of course, I should have told you about it, yet I guess you, too, have to think about it.

"Of course reports on your good work keep coming in to me, and I am glad to hear them. As a matter of fact, I was planning to go to see you one of these days, but something always pops up to keep me from going. I heard you were zealous and I kept telling myself, tomorrow for sure. Well, I suppose that is why I make these slips. That's why I have to make self-criticism so often. So I've slipped again."

His words hurt me sorely. If he had hit me it would have been better. I wished the ground would open and swallow me. After a short pause he went on:

"Comrade Hyong Jin, you and I must know this. To do anything—let it be study or some project—we have to know the people we work with. Particularly, people like Ok Ju and Sung Jae. I think we cannot do anything if we don't know such people.

"I imagine if you stay longer you will be hearing a lot of things. But it is important for the Party members to have a correct understanding of the people they are dealing with. You should not depend on rumors that fly into your ears at the well or in office corners. We must think more about people. All Party members, particularly, a doctor like you, or a Party worker like me, must imbue ourselves with the great leader's ideas, his warm solicitude for man."

The propaganda department instructor returned with a portable radio, still in its wrapping. I saw at once that it was a good radio. The Party chairman, with a broad smile, unpacked the carton and took out the radio. He took a good look at it with childlike curiosity.

"I had meant to get a good radio for him long ago, but not until now had I been able to find one. I would have got a bigger one for sure, but it would have been very clumsy for him. After all, he is bed-ridden. Would you mind taking it to him when you go?"

The chairman carefully packed the portable again and handed it over to me. Then returning to our conversation he took up where he had left off.

"Since you know nothing about these people I will try briefly to tell you about them.

"Sung Jae is a good fellow. He is a recipient of the Order of National Flag First Class and he was awarded two Orders of Soldier's Honour. He became a Party member at the front. During the war he was in an anti-tank team and he knocked off a dozen or so American tanks single-handed. Then he was wounded by splinters from enemy shells. Around the waist, it seems.

"Since his discharge he has received treatment at a number of hospitals for several years, but with little success. His case is regarded as a serious one.

"According to doctors, his case belongs to the category—tuberculosis of bones—you mentioned a few minutes ago, and it is a miracle that he is still alive. But Sung Jae is very optimistic, no less than a healthy person. And the Party too has sent him lots of tonics.

"They got to know each other at the front. Ok Ju was a nurse then. She sees things in a different light from some doctors. She went to medical school to become an assistant doctor because she wanted to save her comrade in revolution. We are proud of this Party member. In the end she married him, yes, she married him whom doctors said would be an invalid for the rest of his days.

"When Ok Ju was discharged she took him to her house—by this time he had had his fill of hospitals. Sung Jae can't do a thing for himself.

"I was at his place some time ago. His wounds were still discharging. As I said, Ok Ju has to do everything for him. She cleanses the wounds; she bathes him, and feeds him. It seems there is little she can do now as far as his condition is concerned, though she finished a medical school. But what can she do? After all, a case like his has been written off as hopeless by many renowned surgeons, I hear. That's why more than ever I hope your research will be successful. I do feel the spirit of the heroic Korean people should be shown in the medical field, too. Where all others fail, Korean doctors should be different.

"The question is devotion, a warm heart for man. Some have doubts as to Ok Ju's motive in marrying him. They view her marriage as something like a beautiful story, a kind act of the simple-minded young girl. It will be seen if they are right.

"On our part, however, we support the couple with all our hearts, we should do everything to help them make a happy home. We wish them all the happiness in the world. Theirs is an unusual, yet very precious home.

"I am sorry that you knew nothing about this family. You are a department head. But I am sure you will from now on, as a Party member, feel responsible for this family."

Tears came to my eyes. I was too moved by the county Party chairman's story to say a word. At no time had I ever heard of such a strong manifestation of love for human beings. It was the very answer that I had been searching for ever since I returned from the war. I was convinced that the human mind can be stronger than medicine; and no doctor has any right to commit such a mind to death.

When I returned to the hospital I gave the radio to Comrade Ok Ju, saying little. I guess I was too overwhelmed. And she was as pleased as Punch with the radio, saying repeatedly she did not know how to thank the county Party chairman. My heart was too full to remember all she said.

That night I could not go to sleep. The bright, radiant face of Ok Ju flashed before my eyes. Who would have ever guessed the heart of this girl playing like a child with a white mouse was such a deep, boundless sea of love? I recalled the night the hospital celebrated the holiday: how she thrilled the people with her singing! Then there was Ok Ju who looked so greatly disturbed. Now I could see what I had thought beautiful of her was only surface—only a particle of Ok Ju, beautiful thorough and thorough, inside and outside. I felt ashamed of my biased outlook. But equally I was overjoyed at the fact that there was such a noble soul beside me.

While I kept tossing from side to side, there was a sudden knock at my door. It was the nurse on duty. A knock at that unearthly hour was no surprise, of course, it is a normal part of a doctor's life. But sensing it was urgent, I hurried to the hospital. My fears were confirmed.

The patient was a woman who had been brought on a cart from some eight kilometres away. Already hospital staff had gathered, Ok Ju among them.

The patient was in considerable pain, and I examined her at once. It was a perforated gastric ulcer. In the layman's language her stomach would soon be punctured, and she had to be operated on at once. But our hospital was not staffed or equipped for major operations. Above all, there was no blood bank for transfusions. It was the standing rule that such cases should be sent to a hospital in the provincial centre. The ambulance was ready to take her there, but it was clear she could not last that long. Something had to be done then and there. I could not say I was an expert at such operations, but in that situation I suggested operating right away. They sent for me and they had expected something of me. In the meantime various tests had been made on the patient. Now another bottleneck. The blood test showed that her blood was "O". Only one person, a woman who had just given birth had "O" group blood. This "O" group is a funny thing. It can be safely given to any one. But "O" group patients have to have "O" group blood.

My blood group is also "O". So I was obviously meant to be a surgeon. But everyone ruled against me. Their argument was this. I was going to operate. What would happen if I gave hundreds of grams of blood? But the situation was urgent. What would happen to the groaning woman while we were arguing?

In the end, I won. Now the whole hospital began to move. Everyone was assigned their position for the operation, and soon everything was ready. Then I rolled up my sleeve and held out my arm. Ok Ju, who was to be my assistant, took out 200 grams of blood from me.

She was very hesitant injecting the needle into my arm, she

looked guilty about the whole thing. But I gently persuaded her until she did as she was told. Bowing her head, she said in a faint voice:

"I'm really sorry to do this!"

The husband or mother of the patient could not have been more sincere than she. She is such a woman—a beautiful woman ready to sacrifice her life for a disabled man, yet she feels pain at taking out a few grams of another's blood. She acted as if it was all her fault!

When I think of her pure heart, I feel I would give the very last ounce of my blood for others.

When she had finished I started on the operation. I soon found out it was a good thing that we had decided to operate on the patient immediately: a little delay would have cost her her life.

She was under the knife for more than four hours. When everything was finished, I was suddenly totally exhausted, me whom you might call a hefty fellow. So you can imagine the condition of the poor woman who had been on the operating table so long. She had lost a lot of blood during operation. She needed another transfusion right away. So I held out my arm again.

Ok Ju just looked at me: I was sweating profusely. In the end, she turned her back on me. I told her to hurry but she just stared at me. So I asked other doctors but no one wanted to do anything. By this time I was very irritated, but pleaded in vain. To think of it now, I guess, I looked pretty bad then. I had been working rather hard for several days. And the four-hour operation and transfusion naturally would make me look haggard. But there was no time to lose. I got angry at everyone, and Ok Ju came round. In a choked voice she said: "I think we must have a blood-bank because there will be other major operations. I really hate to do this." Urged time and again, she finally took out some blood again.

When the patient was sent to the ward, it all really hit me—the feeling of relief and the fatigue. My every joint was aching and I was seeing double. I managed to reach my office and fall into my chair. Then I copped out completely. What a miserable figure I cut! At any rate, some time later—I don't know if it was minutes or hours—I came to. I noticed that the dawn was breaking. Against the brightening window I saw her standing, her worried eyes fixed on me. I felt so awkward that I jumped to my feet and walked home with her in the early hours.

It was a pleasant walk, and our hearts were light, like the time when we met for the first time under the zelkova tree.

I told her I'd like to examine her husband. In the course of conversation I explained to her—and I must confess I exaggerated a little—about my studies. She was childlike in her happiness. She laughed, then she shook her head.

"You know, doctor! I was so afraid of you at first. How foolish of me! You are a good man.... But why did you stare at me like that at our first meeting when you came here?"

It would have been most painful to answer her. I was in trouble again. But, thank heavens, it was not yet light, and I could hide my feelings with a laugh.

"So, you were afraid of me, eh? Maybe I am that kind. Who knows?"

After a moment I resumed:

"One day I'll tell you why I stared at you like that. I'm sure the day will and must come."

At my words she gave me a puzzled look that seemed to say, "I am more confused than ever."

But I must say this. That early morning walk straightened out the delicate, in a way painful, relation between her and me.

And that was one of the most memorable events in my whole life.

The next evening I went to see Sung Jae. Of course, I went with Ok Ju.

Theirs was a charming tile-roofed house at the foot of the mountain. The kitchen was in the middle with a room on either side—one for Ok Ju and her mother, the other, with the earthen porch, for Sung Jae.

The girl's family is small—her father was killed in the war. She has a married brother in Hamhung. Sung Jae, I learned, comes from a village near the demarcation line, which is now on the other side. When he graduated from mining college, he worked in a mine in Hwanghae Province before he joined the army. So it must have been years since he heard from his family.

When Ok Ju led me into his room I found him in his bed. He

was listening attentively to the radio—the radio the county Party chairman had sent. There were lovely flowers in a vase, the same as the ones I saw when I came to the hospital. And there were many books. The room was rather simply decorated but it showed the hand of warm care in everything. It was a very comfortable room.

Not that I had expected otherwise—Sung Jae did not look good. He had been bed-ridden for several years. But I could tell he was a man of strong build, once a robust fellow, I should say. I felt all the more sorry seeing him in such condition. Yet he seemed cheerful, almost in high spirits.

But the illness was serious. The 11th and 12th thoracic and the 5th lumbar vertebrae were fractured, and bone tuberculosis had set in. On top of this, a splinter was stuck in the worst place possible, in the 12th thoracic vertebra. There had been repeated operations but because the position was so dangerous the surgeons had not dared try to remove the splinter. Perhaps it was pressing or had severed the spinal nerve, or maybe because of the pus—in any case, he was paralysed from the waist down. As the county Party chairman had told me, there were several places of discharges on his body—these places were the "gate to death" as they were called in advanced medical circles.

When I entered his room, he showed little interest. Perhaps he was annoyed at my intruding in the midst of a very interesting programme. Or maybe he had had his fill of doctors and had lost all his illusion about them.

But when Ok Ju introduced me to him he reacted quite differently. He told me he had heard about me through friends, other disabled soldiers. I had treated some wounded veterans, particularly my interest being in the line of articular tuberculosis, regarded as incurable. But he seemed little concerned about his own injuries—he was very reluctant when I said I wanted to examine him.

But I insisted and his waist was unbandaged. The injuries were far worse than I had anticipated and my heart sank. To tell you the truth, it obviously was a hopeless case, but I could not very well tell him that.

As I said, the patient seemed indifferent, only Ok Ju was looking on with anxious eyes. And I was most uneasy. So, what did I do? I hacked a few short dry coughs. I must have looked little different from those quacks of the past who prescribed indigestion pills for everything and for everyone, yet collected huge fees, the dignified hypocrites.

With a solemn face, I began to go carefully through the pile of X-ray films, one by one, examining them under the light. I guess it irritated Sung Jae, because he said:

"Doctor, you don't have to see them all. One will be enough to tell you the whole story. You will note little difference between those taken three years ago and the ones done lately."

"But how do you know all that?" I asked, assuming an air of dignity.

"Of course, I know. I could be as good as many a doctor. And then, poor though she may be we have a doctor, in the family."

"My!" exclaimed Ok Ju, slanting her glance to him. I frowned and turned to her. Then to make the patient believe my authority I declared in a well-measured voice:

"I am afraid you are wrong. No disease remains stationary. Either it becomes worse, or it gets better. Sometimes, I must say, the tempo or degree is so small that it is not noticed by untrained eyes. Nothing is stationary; that is an accepted principle in every science."

What I had told him was simply this: you may not be able to see it, but an experienced person like myself will. But it did not impress Sung Jae much.

"Well, if you say so, I must be getting better. Just the same, if you go through every film like that, you will have to stay up all night."

Of course I knew a patient who had been confined for a long time wanted someone to talk to. I have had many such cases. And the same was true of Sung Jae. There was Ok Ju to help him, but it is not nice to be cooped up day in, day out in a small room like a bird with broken wings. So I thought what he would want was several hours of conversation with me. And I was right. As soon as I had put away the films, he fired:

"Doctor, did you listen to the radio this morning?"

"No, I didn't."

Suddenly Ok Ju began to laugh.

"No, you're not going to tell the doctor about it. Doctor, do you know what? Ever since he got the radio, all he talks about is what he hears over the radio. I'm already tired of it now."

"I tell you, you are wrong on that," Sung Jae was blunt. He continued:

"You think what you're doing is everything. But that's wrong, I'm telling you. One must know, and thoroughly too, how reconstruction is going on in Pyongyang where the great leader is, and how the Three-Year Plan is being carried out in all fields of the national economy—how else can one be a good Party member.

"I heard a mine manager making a self-criticism—this morning and he was good. Though he had shown little interest in getting things needed by the miners in their work, it had been an entirely different story when it came to his office. And he did set up his office very nicely. Then whenever the miners failed to fulfil the quotas—when he had neglected to give the miners decent conditions to work in, he had the men on the carpet. Let me tell you, if I know any such manager still around, I would write to the Party Central Committee or to the Heavy Industry Ministry. But as to you, what you are thinking is this—there are no such bureaucrats in your hospital. Oh, no? I'll bet there are. It seems to me you people drive the nurses and attendants needlessly at times, and make little effort to teach them, and little do you care what things are like for them. Yet you think what I'm saying is a big joke!"

"Nobody said it was a joke. Only I said you should not get so heated about it. After all, you may have heard it, but there are many who didn't. Doctor, do you know what he did this morning? He coaxed me into solving a children's riddle that he heard over the air."

It was a pleasant argument. Yes, it warmed my heart. I was so happy that tears almost came. The warmth of the human heart which I had so long forgotten was coming back to me. I was experiencing a new world—a world that my limited sense of measurement could not fathom.

That night I stayed at their place until late and talked. His medical problems "forgotten," the three of us talked about the April Plenary Meeting, the rebuilding of Pyongyang and about lots of things. We attacked the bureaucratic manager of the mine. You know there were still plenty of bureaucrats around in those days.

Sung Jae, as I said, was in a pretty bad state as far as his physical condition was concerned. But spiritually he was buoyant, far more so than I had expected.

He had all the latest news on the developments in the country at his finger tips. Sometimes he laughed heartily, sometimes he was enraged over something. I was particularly impressed by his inexhaustible energy and his devotion. He was studying a new tunneling method which all mining industries could use. As I said, his room was well stocked with books.

I could not help recalling the words of the county Party chairman. He was right when he said that it was the duty of every Party member to make such a home as that of Sung Jae and Ok Ju happy. And I resolved to put him on his feet again so that the whole world might see this family happy.

After that night, my visits to their home became more frequent. If I could not go, Ok Ju brought me a report of her husband's condition; naturally I came to see more of her and to walk with her still more often. And she helped with my work in every way she could. Perhaps the rumour that you had heard started around this time.

With bated breath I listened to my friend as to a testimony read in court. Then I tried to picture the face of Ok Ju, whom I had never met. Yet she was no stranger; I felt I must have seen her in some place—she must have been among the many wonderful Chollima riders whom I met in connection with my news reporting.

We did not notice that the wind had blown itself out, that the sky had become overcast. Only one or two dim stars were visible low in the eastern sky. The moon had vanished altogether. The sky looked threatening over the bright Songyo district across the river—it seemed that it would pour down any minute. The river was still rustling. From somewhere came the cry of a night bird.

After looking round, Hyong Jin continued.

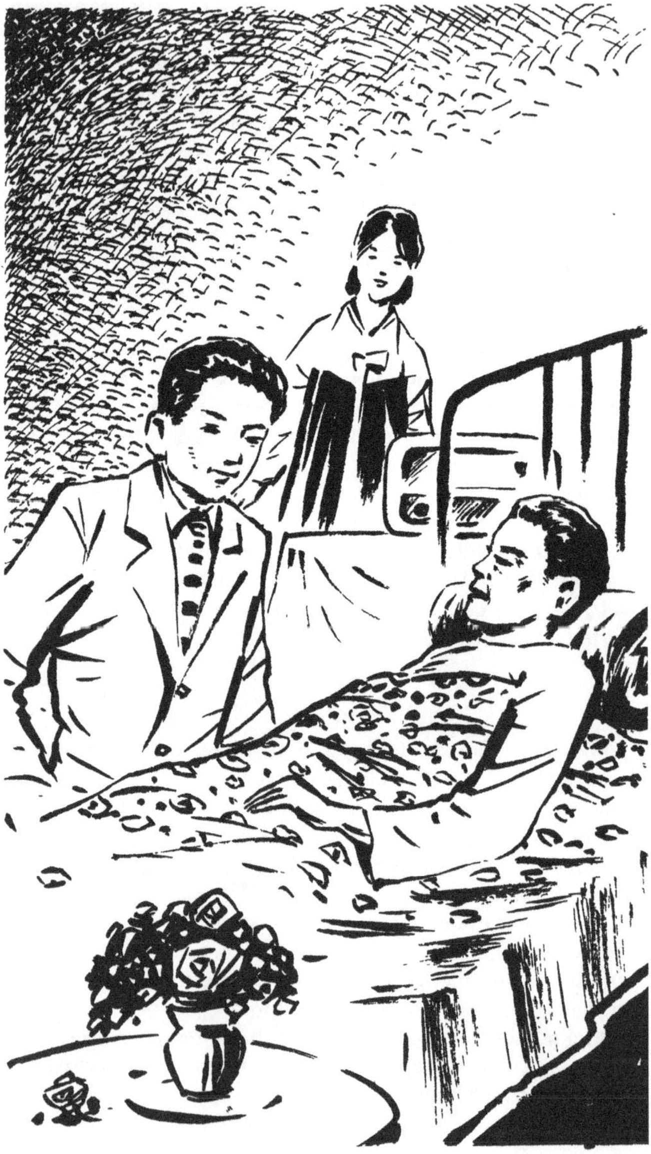

To be honest with you, even then I was not capable of clear thought. Ok Ju's nobility of spirit was almost awesome. Yet, I could not shake off the notion that her motive was not beyond what we call a personal self-sacrifice or a sense of duty. Don't get me wrong—I respected her just the same.

But I was quite sure there must be something overshadowing their life. I knew it would torment me and I tried to avoid seeing it, or I did not want to pry into the depth of their affairs. Both Sung Jae and Ok Ju possessed willpower and reason. Indeed, no one could surpass them in this respect, of that I was sure. But, after all, they are mortal beings. Could they live by will and reason alone? There would be times when human emotions would drive them. Then wouldn't they feel moments of frustration and distress?

And at these thoughts my heart contracted. I meditated. I would find a haven in my work, in hurrying on with my studies. I would cure many people of articular tuberculosis, and, above all, Sung Jae.

I forgot everything in my research project. The field I began to explore was more or less untrodden in the modern medical world. Naturally there were many false starts. Whenever I came up against a knotty problem, I thought about the happiness of Sung Jae and Ok Ju.

It was around this time that my attention began to turn to the bone transplantation in treating articular tuberculosis. And I began to look for possibilities. But there were many barriers, even theoretically.

One night I went to their home again. It was quite late as I had had a lot of work to do.

Meanwhile summer gave way to autumn, the clear autumn that poets sing about.

The moon was very bright and the breeze was gentle. I stepped into their yard, but stopped short. I heard singing! I looked up at the room. The shadow of Ok Ju in traditional dress was on the screen door. She and Sung Jae were singing.

> *The night is lovely!*
> *The breeze is sweet,*
> *The moon is bright.*
> *Come, all my friends,*

> *We will sing merrily.*
> *We will dance joyously.*

It would not have been at all strange if that song had come from a park or from a brightly-lit club. But this song of youth.... Yet, it carried a feeling of joy—as merry as a song that might flow from a club.

You see, listening to them, I thought—or putting it more correctly, I worried that there might be clouds in their life. But how beautiful their song was!

The gentle autumn breeze touched the screen door on which an image of Ok Ju was cast obviously wearing her beautiful traditional Korean dress. Then the deep resonant voice of Sung Jae, wafted out to the silvery sky, while the clear notes of Ok Ju rippled and danced like a happy lark soaring in the boundless heavens.

Immeasurably high are the heavens! The lark's song rose, her dreams were beautiful, her hopes were many.

The melody rolled on, a sweet melody of youth and love. The heavens were boundless, free from all obstacles. The lark can fly and fly. Happiness is the birthright of the lark.

The lark in the clear sky—this was what their joyous song was like. But there was more to it—far more. There was something strong and appealing in their song. It was a piece of art itself, perfect art, to which no painter or composer could do justice. It was a product of the life of our heroic people.... Standing there, I could see their radiant faces filled with happiness.

Their song was beautiful, it was a call to life, an expression of the noblest sentiments of human hearts, reaching the ethereal point of art, a song of true art. For the first time, I was convinced she loved Sung Jae from her heart, not out of sympathy or a sense of duty. And Sung Jae was worthy of her love in every way.

Quietly I turned around. I saw myself as common by comparison with this noble couple. I saw that their love was a modern miracle, and were it for such love, one would not fear to block the muzzle of the enemy's gun with one's own body.

I said to myself that no longer should bone transplant be permitted to be to me the impossible. Now my main thought was that, when it had been achieved, even the hunchback could stand straight! It seemed to me that that day was now in sight. And with happy thoughts I turned and went.

Walking along the night road I thought about true love, about good work, about the happiness of our times.

I ask you once again, what is happiness?

It dawned on me then happiness is not gratification of one's desires. I still firmly believe this—true happiness is not what we have gained but the long hard struggle for it.

If happiness is what the ordinary people think it is, how can we understand the great happiness that our great leader felt when he fought devotedly for the liberation of the country under those hard conditions through snowstorms over the crags of Mt. Paekdu? Then, think of our guerrillas who fought the Japanese imperialists. Do you remember the fighters who went through unspeakable hardships for one or two months for wounded comrades in the depth of the snow-covered forest?

The revolution was a crucial struggle but all could visualize a bright morrow. For this they could face any pain and hardship, some even gave their lives for it. But in every heart there was a sense of profound happiness.

Of course, you recall what hero Li Su Bok, a lad of 18, said when he stopped an enemy machine gun: "No happiness is greater than dedicating one's life and youth to the country." His words seemed to be ringing in my ears.

But so far the human race has faced limitations in every way, socially and historically, to attain the fullest happiness. Only that grows and becomes enriched with time. The present, the era of the Workers' Party, is essentially different from every preceding era, it is an era of great happiness. Why? Because, first of all, the great leader has established an advanced socialist system where everyone plays their part in the battle for social progress, where everyone, creating happiness, enjoys happiness.

Such is our society today. But we should not forget that though today is good, tomorrow will be better still.

The better morrow—what a lovely ideal! Because of this belief, human beings have never ceased to turn the wheel of history. They have never stopped creative activities. In short, we people are on a constant march toward a greater, happier morrow. We have come a long way on this march. At every stage of history we draw closer, step by step, to perfect happiness, communism. From this, it follows that happiness is measured in every stage by one's contribution to this eternal march of the human race, in other words, by how much one has done for social progress in a given period. So I can say now, happiness is not what one has gained, it is an eternal process.

Compared with the old days, our life today, since the liberation, is bountiful beyond measure. But what we have gained is only the starting point for greater happiness. So the Party indicates a new goal for us to reach, rich though we already are. Hence the unflagging zeal for building communism and our Party's idea of continuous revolution. We have taken over the undivided loyalty to the great leader from our anti-Japanese forerunners, and it is our duty to hand it down to the next generation along with a revolutionary concept of happiness. This is the demand of our times and happiness must be seen in it.

In the depth of my heart I felt the happiness of Sung Jae and Ok Ju. It gave me joy that I, too, could enjoy true happiness.

If you can grasp what I felt then, I am sure you can understand why I am telling you all this.

There was a short pause in his talk which left me with a chance to draw a deep breath. He and I had been childhood friends, but I could not listen to him without pain and shame.

As if from nowhere, a young couple passed by. They must have come from the direction of Taedong Gate—we had not noticed their approach because we were so engrossed. The young man must be feeling warm —his jacket was unbuttoned, but the girl had her coat collar turned up. Paying us little attention (I suspect they never even saw us), they went whispering on their way.

I wondered, what they were talking about so fondly at this hour of the night? Were they, too, talking about happiness? Then, what were their thoughts? They might not know the profound happiness that my friend was talking about. I dare say their happiness is much simpler and more clearly delineated. I envied them. For their happiness the older generation fought and toiled, though to them the very battle was happiness. I only hope that what the young people are thinking about is not so earthly and coarse as I once thought.... Suddenly they burst into ringing laughter, as if laughing at me for my foolish worries.

"Well, that's all there is to be said. Shall we go back?"

Throwing the cigarette end into the river, Hyong Jin got up off the bench. We began to walk slowly homeward. In a leisurely manner he resumed:

It took me four years to prepare for the operation. During these years I had some degree of success in treating articular tuberculosis. Newspapers gave more space than I deserved. You know it, so I don't need to tell you about that. Only this. In the beginning, I confess it, I was really groping in the dark, but eventually I succeeded in opening up the bone and using there an antibiotic for bone regeneration. At that time I wrote a paper for a medical magazine—eventually that became the dissertation for my qualification of assistant doctor. It was, no doubt, a major step forward.

The song that I had heard Sung Jae and Ok Ju singing that night helped me find a method of curing spinal cases. As you know, I succeeded in filing off the decayed bone and transplanting a piece of bone marrow.

I operated on many cases, both mild and very serious cases, before I took Sung Jae to hospital. That was in 1960.

This was all he said about the four years—the difficult four years, of which I knew so well. His talk was mostly about Sung Jae and Ok Ju. Of course I knew him; he did not go in for boasting. I had often heard that my colleagues had a lot of trouble with him when they pestered him for information on his work. He would tell them there was little to be said. So they sometimes asked me to help them, knowing Hyong Jin was close to me.

Yet, we could report enough on his research to give a general picture to our readers. There were numerous articles about him—how he designed special instruments, how they were made (he visited factories so often), how he took out his own as an experiment before he operated on patients....

Knowing his turn of mind, I did not coax him into telling me any more about those difficult years. I let him talk about Sung Jae's operation. He described it:

Stories about operations are never entertaining, and Sung Jae's case was one of the worst of all, a very serious case. Figuratively speaking, his was a house without a pillar! The operation took almost the whole day. A dozen or so people were assigned to help, and the whole hospital's attention was focussed on it.

Before the operation the entire hospital staff read together the story of "The Surgeon of the Guerrillas" from *The Reminiscences of the Anti-Japanese Guerrillas*. I must tell you this, too. The county Party chairman, who was in Pyongyang on business, rang us up to encourage us.

When the appointed hour came, I went into the operating theatre with a great sense of responsibility. Ok Ju was there with a hemostat, and I could feel her eyes following me, those clear, bright talking eyes. I tried not to look at her face as I started the first incision.

Soon the pus was cleared, and the pleurae were removed, and the infected part where the cursed Yankee shell splinter had lodged was exposed. My hands began to tremble because I realized once again that I was handling the dear life of a human being, not a house of logs. I had to use the file—the most difficult part was that with one hand I had to press down his back so that I could work the file between the pleurae....

Here I was, and you know how far am I from being dexterous—yet I had to perform such a delicate job. (It had taken me almost a year to get acquainted with the right surgical instruments.)

Now the infected part was cut out, the spine was severed into two, and I could see the ugly piece of splinter. The white spine nerve appeared and disappeared as the patient breathed. That shell splinter had to be removed. If the nerve was caught on it, the splinter would cut it and that would be the end. Suddenly a fear seized me. From the appearance I could not tell whether or not the splinter had eaten into the nerve. Even if it had not, there was still danger ;   it might snap while I was trying to remove the splinter. For ten years Sung Jae had not been able to use his lower limbs, but it remained to be seen if it was the infection or the shell splinter that was preventing them.

Suddenly the patient's breathing became heavy! This meant things were getting more urgent. His whole life hung by that white thread, the nerve. This is the philosophical subject human beings have debated for some twenty centuries— which is more basic, mind or matter. If the nerve snaps, the patient will cease to be a human being. I became desperate, and I cried out in my mind.

"What shall I do, Comrade Leader?"

Now the wind hissed with a greater force over the river. And the sky looked as if it would pour down at any minute. Young trees along the promenade were swaying. We did not notice that we passed by our house. My friend kept talking; he seemed not to notice it.

The penetrating voice of the great leader echoed in my heart.
"Have trust in man and love man!"

Yes, I put trust in Sung Jae's willpower. His steel-like spirit inspired me.

The operation theatre was tense. The anaesthetist administered more ether, and the patient's breathing became even again. I took a firm hold of the ugly piece of splinter and removed it from Sung Jae's spine.

Would you believe me if I tell you that I saw the distorted faces of American war maniacs in that piece of metal? I wish you could have some idea of what a sense of triumph I felt when I picked up the piece with my tweezers. Mentally I cried out: "Thank you, Leader!"

To our great relief, Sung Jae's spine was all right. I guess Sung Jae was simply too much for a Yankee shell! Greatly agitated but calmly and with minute accuracy I put a piece of bone marrow in its place. While this was going on, I knew that all the time Ok Ju's eyes were on me. As for her part in the operation, she was as efficient an assistant as a surgeon could hope to have. Yet, I could tell the operation was overtaxing her heart. She looked almost old, which pained me very much.

After the operation we stayed up four nights. Nobody wanted, and they could not have even if they wanted to rest before they knew the outcome of the difficult operation. Yet, I could not bring myself to walk into his room and find out how the patient was doing. I was afraid in a way. I stayed in my office and they were to let me know right away if there was any "change." Ok Ju stayed with him in the ward. She, of course, was as anxious and uneasy as I was.

It was the fourth night. I sat at my desk staring into space, yet I was all ears. If there was a footstep in the hallway I leaped up and reached for the stethoscope. Heaven knows how many times I had repeated that. But every time the footsteps either passed my door or stopped short of it. What a relief I felt then!

The night was getting late when the stillness of the hallway was suddenly shattered. It sounded like someone almost running down the corridor. Again I jumped to my feet as if shot up by a spring. The footsteps became louder. I hoped they would disappear in some other direction, but they were coming toward me, I could tell.

Clasping my hair, I sank down. I knew, it was Ok Ju rushing to me.

Sure enough the door of my room was flung open; I rose instinctively. Ok Ju stood there a moment without saying anything. When she did speak, her words were almost incoherent: "Doctor, they are moving, moving!" I can't have been exactly alert by that time either. Both of us raced down the corridor to Sung Jae's room. And she kept repeating: "They are moving!"

Standing by Sung Jae's bed, I saw what Ok Ju had meant. His toes, which had been immobilized nearly ten years, were moving! Words failed me.

We all had hoped this would happen, but when it did happen, the impact was too great to bear. Was I to laugh or cry?

Ok Ju, by now well-composed again, stepped forward to stand by me and said in a whisper: "Thank you, Doctor!"

I turned my eyes to her—I almost took her for Kyong Suk again! Her eyes were filled with tears. That was the first and last tears that I saw in her eyes. I realized then what it meant, the moving of Sung Jae's toes. And there was a lump in my throat, too. So I hurriedly left the patient's room.

My friend breathed heavily now as if he had just come out of Sung Jae's room. Then, he noticed where we were. Laughing heartily he said.

Look where we are! Let's go back home. Looks like it's going to pour. At any rate, my story is finished. But I must add this. After that I saw Ok Ju helping her husband to stand on his feet again. How merry her laughter sounded. How cheerful and peaceful she looked, she was free from all worries. I thought nature was extremely prejudiced to her to endow her with such beauty. In her I saw all the noble features of a Korean woman.

Before long Sung Jae walked out of the hospital toward happiness and communism. Yes, he walked out of the hospital!

Last autumn they were formally married. They had set a date convenient for the county Party chairman and for me, who had to be in Pyongyang to attend the Party Congress. But, to my regret, there was a meeting after the Congress at which I had to be present. It was a conference of the Academy. So I was unable to get to their wedding, but I sent them a long message, a most sincere one.

I hear the county Party chairman got quite excited that day. You know he is a serious man, but he sang folk songs in his own accent, dancing to the tune! They say his eyes were moist the whole time.

Sung Jae was given a new assignment and he and Ok Ju left the town. They sent me their wedding photographs and I sent them ours. Looking at the image of my wife who rather resembled Ok Ju, the latter perhaps came to see why I had stared at her when we had the first meeting. For reply they wrote a long letter. I suppose that kind of letter is what we call a letter from the heart.

Now Sung Jae is working in a mine, where he went to

advance the mining industry. The ore he mined will feed our industry, and our industry will enrich our lives.

I can almost say now this is all I wanted.

While you were reporting on the exploits of the builders of Okryu Bridge, I was preparing my instruments for the operation. When you wrote about the unveiling of the Chollima Statue I wrote the discharge papers for Sung Jae.

And I leave it to you to write the conclusion.

Since you are interested in it, you'd better know this as well. About my personal affairs, there will be something to tell pretty soon. So you don't need to worry about that any longer. It seems the county Party chairman did a lot of propaganda work on my behalf. Believe me, there have been a lot of possibilities.

But somehow I am a sort of bystander and the county Party chairman is doing all the talking, and he is turning down one after another. He is quite hard to please. I hear there is a best one, but he is not sure yet! At any rate, the matter may be settled pretty soon. Perhaps you'd better start looking for a nice present.

In the distance, the Chollima Statue on Mansudae Hill was silhouetted against the dark sky—the image of Chollima dashing at lightning speed. Once more, I looked at my friend, a truly ordinary man of our time! Big drops began to come down. "Here she comes!" With these words he started off in long strides, just like a school boy.

Standing there in the rain, I watched him heading for the house. The early spring shower quickly turned into a downpour. As if to wash away my hazy thoughts. It poured down on the dust-covered shoes, and on the head filled with earthly thoughts.

1963

Ogi

Chon Se Bong

Ogi was 20 years old, though she looked two or three years younger than her age. She was very short and shy and her deep-set eyes were always smiling. Her eyes added charm to her lovely face. She had only finished junior middle school, but she was unusually intelligent.

She took an active part in Democratic Youth League study sessions and agro-technique pass-on meetings. She also read lots of newspapers and magazines and sometimes sat up all the night reading a novel.

Her friends nicknamed her "dove". Partly because her mother had brought her and her elder brother up as peaceful as a pair of peaceful doves, and partly because Ogi was as graceful and as lovely as a dove. Now her brother was a student at Kim Chaek University of Technology.

Anyway, Ogi was a charming girl. All the villagers were so

attached to her, but not just for her looks. She was well known for her diligence. She rarely rested at her work place or at home. She was both dexterous and sensitive.

During the rice planting season she usually planted 600 *pyong* (about 1,000 m²) a day. At home, at the sewing-machine she could easily make a garment in a few hours at night. This winter Ogi had collected more than three tons of manure all by herself.

She didn't like to lag behind others on any job. This morning, for example, she had come to work half an hour earlier than the others. She hurried to the pigsty and pulled down the dung-heap with a rake. She prepared a trailerful of manure well ahead, so that when the tractor came there was no time wasted.

The manure in the pigsties which was trodden in was frozen. To make matters worse, forking was very difficult because some sloppy pig-breeders had not cut up some of the straw spread in the pigpens.

"Ogi is always the first. If everybody worked like Ogi, reaching the production goal, an extra million tons of grain, would be easy. Hand it to me. I'll help you."

The workteam leader who had come unnoticed approached her and snatched up the fork.

"Oh, please don't."

"Hum, there is a fork over there."

The workteam leader caught sight of a fork stood up against the pigsty and went there in a vigorous step.

"Ogi, let's prove our merits in farming this year. We really must not fall behind other villages, must we?"

"Of course not."

Ogi smiled as she dug up the manure.

The lanky workteam leader, too, pulled down the dung-heap energetically.

"Ogi, do you meet Comrade Bong Guk now and then?"

"My goodness!"

Ogi was embarrassed.

"I'm just asking you about your lover, there's nothing surprising in that."

"Please stop your teasing!"

"Teasing? Humph, you are wrong there. You are so shy that

you dare not see Comrade Bong Guk. That's silly of you. You're a model worker and you shouldn't be afraid to meet a man you ought to meet. You're 20, you're a big girl now."

Ogi ran away to another dung-heap, blushing to her ear lobes. The leader laughed aloud. Whenever he saw her he would tease her because Ogi was as cute as a little child. This morning, too, he felt like carrying her on his back and walking about proudly.

Ogi raked the manure down harder than before, her face still flushed. Bong Guk was a tractor driver who lived in Kangbuk-ri, a village across the river. He had ploughed the fields of Ogi's village during the late spring months but in the autumn he had moved to Kangbuk-ri village. In Ogi's village Bong Guk tilled the fields heart and soul. On night shifts, he tilled the ricefields despite the cold rain. Sometimes, at night, he went over to the tractor workshop to have broken chains repaired on his machine.

He was a tough man who helped the farmers out on the heavy jobs.

His devotion quite impressed Ogi. She heard that Bong Guk had only completed junior middle school like her, but he was rather well-informed. Once he had a debate with senior middle school graduates on a subject of chemistry and he proved he knew as much as they did. This also impressed her.

She had never had a date with him; she had happened to meet him and had talked to him at the democratic propaganda hall a couple of times. But Ogi felt shier and her heart throbbed wildly whenever she saw him. God knows why.

Soon after he moved to Kangbuk-ri Bong Guk proposed marriage to her. Her heart was filled with happiness mingled with shyness and her mother didn't hesitate over his proposal. She said that Bong Guk was a real man. Ogi's lover was such a man.

Presently a tractor-trailer arrived in front of the pigsties. A group of girls came out with forks and shovels on their shoulders.

"Oh, Ogi, you are first again, doing so much work again this morning."

"The team leader has done much more than I have."

Ogi didn't like praise. So she said that the team leader had done much more than she, though he had left after digging a little because he had to secure ox-carts to carry humus.

"How many loads shall we have today, Ogi?" Pressing her shovel into the humus, Gye Suk asked in a low voice.

"At least 20."

"But the distance is greater than yesterday."

"So we will have to load and unload more quickly!"

"It's impossible."

"How do you know it's impossible? Let's try!"

Ogi had done a great deal of work, and her face became flushed. Her hot breath looked like steam. She poked her pitchfork into the mass of frozen manure and lifted up and threw it onto the trailer. Though of small build, she was strong. In fact, she was the shortest of the five girls and looked like a child, but she led them in work. She came to work early in the morning, and in the evening, when the day's work was over, she often suggested taking an extra load.

"Look, they say no one can complete his work before entering his grave. Don't your legs feel stiff?"

"Ho, ho, ho. They do. But, girls, come on, just one more load."

She was not dictating but pleading the way a little child does. And the girls had to agree. Some of the girls complained, "You keep on smiling to make us work."

They started to load the trailer again. When it was finally filled with humus, Gye Suk, flinging up the pitckfork, shouted, "Okay, now, Comrade Driver. Go!"

Kim Chi Ho the driver who had been rubbing something with an oil-cloth at a distance nodded and grinned.

The girls got noisily onto the trailer, tools in hand. The tractor started to rattle, pulling its trailer. It was the beginning of February, and winter was past its height, but the weather was very cold. The tractor rumbled out of the village along the ice-covered road. The thin ice was crushed under the wheels. The haze could be seen over the field beyond the causeway. The girls resigned themselves to the shaking of the trailer on which they sat like ducks in a crate. They didn't keep their mouths shut, they chattered on and on like skylarks, laughing, their heads off, at what was said. Once the trailer rolled into the field, they started to sing:

Comrades, be ready, arms in hand.
Advance bravely, unafraid,
Smash the imperialist aggressors.

The chorus rang through the field. They looked as if they were going to the battlefield on a military truck, combat ready. The tractor ran along the field path for a good while, then gradually slowed down. A young man, coming from the opposite direction, was smiling.

"Ogi, here comes your footballer!"

The girls raised a fuss, slapping Ogi's back. The footballer was Bong Guk, Ogi's fiance. He got the nickname because he played well and generally liked sports. Bong Guk himself liked his nickname. At the sight of Bong Guk, Ogi pulled her head in like a turtle.

"What has brought you here? Why are you loafing around at this busy time?" asked Chi Ho, pulling up the tractor, and held out his hand to shake it with his colleague.

"I've got some business. Why did you take away all the nuts made at the repair shop? You are greedy."

"That's a good excuse! You're behaving like a girl who goes weeding her lover's grave on the excuse of picking bellflower roots. Have you really come to get the nuts?"

Kim Chi Ho looked askance at him, pouting his lips. What he meant was "You've come to see Ogi." Bong Guk did not answer, he just went over to the trailer, grinning.

"Aren't you going to shake hands with me, girls?"

He was on nodding terms with all of them because he had worked for them the previous spring.

"Why not? Shake Ogi's hand first." The girls pushed her to the side of the trailer. Ogi pinched their arms furiously.

"What's the matter with you? Why pinch us? We know you'd kiss him if you were alone."

Ogi kept hiding behind their backs. The girls laughed merrily.

"Knock it off! She might fall off."

"Then you can hold her in your arms. You are her lover, you can do it."

"Oh, no! I like coming to this village, but I hate that gaggling goose...." Bong Guk fled towards the cab of the tractor. The gaggling goose meant Gye Suk. The girls held their sides with laughter again.

"I've got something to do in the village. Do me a favour; I need two nuts." Bong Guk said to Kim Chi Ho who sat at the wheel.

"What are you going there for? You've seen your sweetheart. Shake hands with her here. Isn't that enough?"

"Stop teasing. I'll be back."

Bong Guk turned round grinning and walked past the trailer. This time the girls clammed up, only smiling.

"What fearful eyes he has!"

"And his fists as big as a baby's head."

"If he gets angry, he could lift up the tractor and turn it over."

"Oh, you are making Ogi unhappy."

The girls whispered to each other, and burst out laughing again.

Not knowing what the girls were saying, Bong Guk had gone quite on a way, whistling. Ogi only raised her head and looked at the Bong Guk's back when the tractor began to move on and he was quite a way off.

Sitting on the trailer, the girls made more fuss. Gye Suk, the chatterbox, rattled on and on. She said that a cowboy had met a girl weaver, that Master Li had met Chun Hyang, that she wondered when they would have a wedding party, that Ogi would bear a boy child and carry him on her back next spring, and so on. Ogi was powerless before the glib-tongued mischievous girls and only laughed until tears came to her eyes.

The tractor unloaded the manure in the middle of the field and rumbled off. The field was dotted with piles of manure as far as the eye could see. The manure would soon be bubbling in the paddies and thick and sturdy rice stalks would grow and dance this year. Girls started singing again. They had an urge to fly in the air and flutter over the field of clouds, instead of driving across it down on the earth.

"Oh, what the hell is he doing? Is he going to spend the whole day getting his nuts?" said Kim Chi Ho, pulling up his tractor by the pigsties. He repeated this several times. Still Bong Guk didn't turn up, though Kim Chi Ho had made three trips to the field.

"Humph, he always acts as he pleases. How could he be so lazy at a time when every minute, every second is so precious?" muttered Kim Chi Ho irritated, looking at his wristwatch. He had just finished the fourth trip. Ogi had a heavy heart. She waited impatiently for Bong Guk to come. She did not believe that her lover was self-willed or lazy. He is late because he has some business to do, she thought. And yet, she was on edge. So from time to time she raised her flushed face unnoticed, to see if he was coming.

It was already lunchtime when he made his appearance.

"Why, you came here for a couple of spare parts and have been waiting for sunset," protested Kim Chi Ho.

"I couldn't help it."

"Couldn't help it? Well, are you fulfilling your haulage assignment these days?"

"More than one hundred per cent every day. You think you are the only person who overfulfils the plan?"

"Shut up. Don't be so idle; hurry up and get your work done."

Kim Chi Ho remonstrated, with a trace of joke in the tone.

"Hell! These bloody nuts annoy me. Those blokes at the repair shop aren't doing their job properly." Turning a deaf ear to Kim Chi Ho's complaint Bong Guk criticized the farm machine station's repair shop.

"What do you mean by saying that they aren't working properly?"

"Why don't they make enough nuts and bolts? They should give priority to producing spare parts. They ought to distribute the parts evenly to all vehicles or make it a rule to exchange a battered one for a new one. Why can't they do that?"

"That rule has already been made. You can only get a new one when you hand an old one in."

"Then, how come you've got some extra ones?"

"I got them long ago."

"Have you any conscience, working hand in glove with the repair shop people?" Now, Bong Guk got the upper hand of Kim Chi Ho and attacked him. While the young men were blaming each other by the feed storage, the girls hurried to a pigsty where there were new-born piglets, and got to chattering there, instead of going home for lunch.

But Ogi didn't join them. She stole her way around to the back wall of the feed storage, and flattened herself against it to eavesdrop on the young drivers' wrangle. Judging from their arguments, it seemed unlikely that Bong Guk was the sort of person who loafed on the job. He also seemed to be justified in his criticism of the repair shop. She gave a sigh of relief. A wagtail came flying and perched on the eaves. The bird pecked away at the straw with its beautiful bill, waggling its long tail. It caught Ogi's attention. Oh, how lovely! she said to herself. I wonder whether those birds lead the kind of lives human beings do, if they have friends and sweethearts — ha, ha, ha. She watched the wagtail and covered her face with her hands, ashamed at her own desultory thoughts. Bong Guk and Chi Ho left the place after arguing a while. When she got home for lunch, she found her mother in a gloomy mood. What's wrong with her? she wondered.

"Mother, did you do your work today—crushing the baked clay?" asked Ogi.

Her mother had told her that morning that she would go to the work.

"Yes, but while I was working, Bong Guk came to see me, saying that he wanted a word with me, so I returned home with him. I didn't do the work I was supposed to do by noon."

The mother's tone of voice was listless and dejected. What had Bong Guk told her mother to make her so cast down? Ogi thought to herself uneasily.

"You met Bong Guk?"

"N-no, Mother."

"That rascal! These are the busiest days for us all and I just can't understand why he had to spend half a day here for a trifling matter."

"He must have some business to do."

"He has a crooked mind."

"What did he say?"

"Well, he said he would give up his job as tractor driver."

"Why?"

"He said he had chosen the wrong job."

"Wrong job?"

"How silly he is! What's wrong if he works hard as driver? He has got a useful skill. He said he had wasted four years as tractor driver, and he had no possibility of development. What's wrong if he works as driver all his life? Surely there is nothing more useful than helping the farmers with machines. There is no distinction in jobs in our country today. Work at any post, and you'll become a hero, a person of importance."

Her mother was hot-tempered by nature but apparently she had dared not say a word to her future son-in-law, and, now was venting her anger on her daughter.

"Oh, Mother."

Head bowed, Ogi scratched at the earthen top of the kitchen range with her fingernail.

"I'm afraid I've overestimated him. As the saying goes, you can sound water ten fathoms deep, but you can't sound man's mind a single fathom. It can't be helped."

Ogi remained silent.

"He brought material for his shirt and trousers and before taking leave he scribbled a few words for you on the desk. You'll find the note in the drawer."

Mother was still cross and she heaved a sigh. Ogi fished out the material and an envelope with a slip of paper in it. She turned her back on her mother and opened the envelope.

"What does he say?"

Ogi did not answer. Her face was clouded.

The letter confirmed what her mother had said. It said after finishing junior middle school he had learned how to drive a tractor, and had found his life worthwhile; but nowadays, that feeling was changing and he had realized that he had taken the wrong road; that many of his schoolmates whom he had thought to be less bright than he had gone to universities last autumn through senior middle school; he had recently received many letters from them and been hardly able to soothe his burning heart; therefore, he had decided to quit his job soon and start preparing to go to a university; and he was shortly going to his home village and he would appreciate it if she made his shirt and trousers quickly.

"I should have chided him harshly. I just listened meekly to what the changeable fellow said. I was to blame."

The daughter's serious look caused her to feel remorse for her failure to remonstrate with her future son-in-law.

Ogi lay wide awake that night. For the life of her, she

couldn't understand why such a hard-working youth was talking such absurdities. Now that the mechanization of agriculture had become so urgent, Bong Guk should be aware of the importance of his job, she thought to herself. But he is going to leave his job. What does that mean? Perhaps I have thought too well of him; maybe I mistook him for a good man, though he was not sincere. She was greatly vexed and disappointed. And yet, she didn't want to blame him for his stupid idea. Bong Guk is my man, after all, she reasoned. I'm the nearest person to him, am I not? These thoughts kept gnawing at her heart. She sat up on bed running her fingers through her hair. The moonlight streamed into the eastern window, on which the shadow of the branches of the apple tree standing by the fence hung, like a picture. It reminded her of that moonlit night last autumn when Bong Guk came to her home. He had put his huge hand on her shoulder by the nearby stream. How ashamed and bewildered she had been! Tears welled up in her eyes.

The co-op farm had more and more work to do now. The farmers busied themselves in an endeavour to bring in ten tons of rice per hectare from all the paddies this year. Therefore, they were so engrossed in the production of animal manure and the improvement of the field. Ogi's team had already carried 50 more tons of fertilizer into each hectare of their field. The team members, however, insisted on applying another 50 tons and more fertilizers. Meanwhile, the farm had got down to the business of levelling some 20 hectares of paddy fields in the gully. Once these fields were put into good shape, giant six-blade plow tractors could till the whole of the cultivated area. Hence the co-operative farm had requested the farm machine station to help with the project. Using the tractors sent at their request, Ogi and her girl friends had buckled down to carrying out the soil brought from other places to improve the fields.

She was plagued with anxiety for a few days. One day after supper, Ogi headed for the farm management board's office, trying not to be noticed. She found it hard to hold herself aloof from her lover's affairs. When she got to the office, she found electric light streaming out of the window. Ogi stood on tiptoe to peep into the room. There was only the chief bookkeeper with a slender neck writing something at his desk. She had come to use the telephone, but she was shy and hesitated to get in.

"Well, what if the chief bookkeeper pokes fun at me?"

Leaning against the wall she held her breath, and again she looked into the room through the window. The chief bookkeeper was lighting a cigarette. Thinking that she needn't be hesitant, she cautiously stepped up to the doorway, opened the door quickly and entered the room. As the chief bookkeeper stared at her, she covered her mouth with her hand.

"Oh, it's you, Ogi. You are smiling again. Whenever you meet people, you smile."

"What's wrong with smiling?"

"Who said it's wrong? Who in the world would blame you who are in the happiest moments of your life."

"Dear me!"

She smiled, her face crimson.

"What do you want?"

"To make a phone call."

"A phone call? You're a big girl, indeed. Making a telephone call...."

"Ho, ho, ho...."

Ogi made for the table on which the telephone was laid, lifted the receiver and dialed the number.

"Hello, will you put me through to Kangbuk-ri, please?"

Once she mustered up courage, there was a change in her mood and she got excited.

"Is that Kangbuk-ri? No, I mean the Kangbuk-ri management board."

Ogi had seldom handled a telephone and was clumsy with the receiver, and she put her mouth almost into the mouthpiece and shouted at the top of her high-pitched voice.

"Ogi, keep your lips further away from the mouthpiece. If you speak with your mouth so close to it, the person at the other end will have trouble hearing you."

"Ho, ho, ho...."

The girl's face grew redder, and showed a sign of confusion.

"Hello, Kangbuk-ri? Well, the chief bookkeeper asked me...."

"Oh, dear, you are using my name, instead of telling them who you are?!"

With a smile on his face, he gazed at her having a hard time with the telephone.

"The chief bookkeeper asked me to phone for him. Yes, that's right. Is the tractor driver in? Don't you know him? Kim Bong Guk. Just left there? My goodness! Would you find him and bring him to the phone? Ho, ho, ho...."

"Hum, you're grown up enough to ring your lover." These frolicking words had no effect on the girl. She strained her ears pressed against the receiver to listen for a voice. Beads of sweat stood on her nose.

"Yes. What? Is it Comrade Kim Bong Guk? This is Ogi."

She bent over the table to put the telephone closer to her.

The hem of her skirt swayed around the leg of the table.

"Hello, I have got something to tell you. Pardon? No, I can't tell you here now. Could you come over to the riverside? Yes. Be sure to come."

After hanging up the receiver she paused for some moments.

"Ogi, you really are grand. You even make no scruple of ordering your man to come to the riverside in such businesslike manner."

The chief bookkeeper was still grinning. But Ogi made no reply, her mouth pursed up. Beads of perspiration gleamed on her forehead, too. She left the office room, and hastened her steps to the riverside. Her heart thumped wildly. She got to the riverside to find that Bong Guk was not there. He would, in all probability, be on the opposite side of the river waiting for her. She felt shy at the thought of seeing him. She bit her lips, and promptly stepped on the ice, which cracked under her weight. As the ice was not hard enough, she might slip into the water. But Ogi was not frightened. The wind wasn't cold. She even felt as if hot water were splashing at her face. Ogi slid on the ice to the far side of the river. The moment she set her foot on the bank, she saw a dark figure treading towards her. It was Bong Guk. He had just got there.

"What do you want to see me for?" asked Bong Guk with a smile, walking up to Ogi who was so small that she stood up to his armpit.

She remained standing without a word. She was scared stiff.

"Did you read the letter I left in the desk drawer?"

"I did," answered she in a faint voice.

"As I wrote in my letter, I decided to quit my bloody job. Honestly, I was too young when I graduated from middle school, I chose a wrong road on a whim."

"On a whim?"

"That's right. Prompted by my spirits I should have thought about my future more seriously."

"I don't understand you. I wanted to talk to you about just that. How could you possibly regret choosing such a useful job as a mere result of a whim? To my mind, you are thinking that way because you have got a fickle heart."

"What? A fickle heart?"

"Yes. Exactly. A fickle heart. Vanity. Indeed, you are out of your mind."

Ogi's voice became louder and louder. She was bashful, but that depended on circumstances. She was another girl when talking along with him.

"Out of my mind?"

"You are. That's why you told a lie the other day that you had come to borrow nuts from the driver of our village. I know it. You are behaving at your own will, carried away by vanity."

"Well said. Speak your tongue out."

"It may be disgusting to you, but hear me out. In my opinion, no occupation is more honourable than tractor driving. Because it is the working-class assistance to the peasant. As a matter of fact, we cannot say that a tractor driver merely ploughs the fields for farmers with his machine. His is a very honourable job."

"What about it?"

The more he listened to her, the sharper and more reasonable the words she uttered. He had never imagined that she would say such things. Though Bong Guk was engaged to Ogi, he had always regarded her as a child. So he had thought that he only had to speak about any matter and Ogi would follow him meekly like a sheep. In short, Bong Guk had treated her lightly.

"I want to learn more. Is it bad?"

"Of course not. But you have a lot of chances of learning while driving a tractor."

"Nonsense. What could you learn by driving it? Do you think you could learn as much as in university?"

"Why not? It depends on your enthusiasm."

"Don't try to draw a rosy picture. I know as well as you do. I feel frustrated at the thought of my backwardness. But you are preaching to me to study while driving a tractor."

"You are wrong there. I think you are more progressive than your schoolmates. That's why you came to the countryside, to drive a tractor. How honourable. But you don't understand your situation or your honourable mission, you've just got your head in the air. Why do you think you're backward? You're wrong. For goodness' sake, get away from the nonsense. Sometimes one may be guided by a wrong idea. But, if one overcomes it, it becomes all right."

"Stop your preaching."

Bong Guk was obstinate, but Ogi felt so sorry that her eyes were filled with tears. Bong Guk realized that he hadn't understood her real personality. It had seemed to him that she was so small and slight that she would be for ever under his thumb, but now he couldn't understand where she had kept such power and audacity.

"Oh, have you come here to preach at me?"

"I'm not preaching. I've come as I feared that you might have got a wrong idea."

"You've got a childish view. That's what I think."

"However childish it may be, please listen to me. Otherwise, I really won't...."

"Won't what?"

"I really don't know what to do, if you stick to such an attitude."

"I don't care whether you don't know what to do or not."

"Good gracious...."

Bong Guk remained for a while, before he threw the half-smoked cigarette at the water's edge. Red sparks scattered in the wind.

"All right. It's no use talking any more."

He disappeared into the darkness. Ogi's legs trembled. She thought she was wronged by him. She had a broken heart. Ogi walked dejectedly across the river in the darkness. She was very sad.

How can I rid him of his vanity? Ogi wondered. I must save him by all means.

She had heard at study sessions of Democratic Youth League and lecture meetings that one can be reformed to be a communist and a Chollima rider. Kil Hwak Sil and many other Chollima riders had been mentioned and praised. There is no reason why Bong Guk cannot be reformed when so many people are reeducated, Ogi thought to herself. I should help him take the right road. I'll help him!

Her mind was preoccupied with these thoughts all the night.

The following day she wrote a letter in haste to her brother who was studying at Kim Chaek University of Technology. In the letter she asked about the necessary formalities to take the university's correspondence course, the date of the examinations of the applicants and the admission requirements. She was anxious to settle Bong Guk down to his work and enable him to take a collegiate course as he wished.

One evening Ogi was coming back with Gye Suk from field-levelling, when Bong Guk rose to his feet abruptly under the zelkova tree near the causeway in front of the village. He must have been to Ogi's as he was holding a roll of cloth in his hand. It was the material for the shirt and trousers. In fact, Ogi had had no time to make his clothes. She felt a chill when she saw him coming towards her with the material in his hand. Bong Guk looked awfully gruff.

Gye Suk was glad to see him and said hello to him, but he completely ignored her.

"I want to meet you, Ogi," Bong Guk grumbled, and went slowly down the slope.

"What's the matter with him? Anything happened?" Gye Suk whispered to Ogi.

"No...."

"Then, what does he mean? Go see him."

Gye Suk pushed Ogi forward. Then Gye Suk herself stealthily left the road. Turning round the zelkova tree she went up to a thicket above the slope where she squatted down. Bong Guk was seated down below with his back towards her.

Bong Guk's attitude was so strange that she decided to overhear what he was going to say. She looked down. The young man remained seated, not so much as looking at Ogi coming to his side. He was wearing a cotton padded jacket and his shoulder looked as broad as a span of both arms stretched. Ogi was two years younger than Bong Guk, but she looked far too young. At this very moment, Bong Guk looked like a giant bee, while Ogi, for her timidity, resembled a frail red-pepper flower.

"Have you been to my home?" Ogi spoke first.

"I have."

"I'm sorry I had no time to make your clothes."

"That's all right. What's the use of making me clothes? It's none of your business, so you needn't bother about them."

Bong Guk placed the rolled cloths negligently under his buttocks and sat down on them.

"Dear me...."

"Today your mother told me many nice things. Now I think I understand how your mother and you think about me and how you are treating me."

"What do you mean by treating?"

"As your mother and you say, I am full of vanity. But, vain or not, I have a viewpoint. Even a man labelled as vain has his logic which may completely refute such a charge. In fact, you don't really understand me, so how could you possibly expect me to marry you?"

His clenched fists were trembling. Ogi could imagine how her mother had reproached him. But she hadn't expected such an explosion from him.

"Calm down and then think it over."

"What? Think it over? And then what?"

"Well, my mother doesn't know you that well. So she got angry and started saying things. And you resent it which you shouldn't. Oh, dear...."

Ogi laughed as if scandalized.

"Don't give me that. You're being silly, and it's very serious. I am not an idiot. Go your way and do as you like."

Bong Guk sprang to his feet and made for the riverside.

Squatting in the thicket, Gye Suk had overheard it all. Her

heart misgave her. She thought Ogi would throw herself to the ground and weep. But she stood still, fixing her eyes on Bong Guk's receding figure.

Gye Suk chased down the slope.

"What did Bong Guk say?"

"Good heavens! You haven't gone home yet." Ogi turned back in surprise. She hastily wiped away the tears in her eyes with her sleeve.

"What did he say?"

"Ho, ho, ho... nothing."

Red-faced Ogi tried to hide what had happened.

"Don't lie to me. I overheard it all. You really are spineless. To listen to him meekly like that! I don't know what your mother said. But how dare he break the engagement, just because he was scolded by his mother-in-law?"

"Don't make such a fuss. He must have been excited. That's why...."

"However excited, nobody calls his father his son. He must distinguish right from wrong even if he is excited."

Gye Suk was as angry as if the matter concerned her directly. Ogi redressed her muffler unnecessarily. Tears welled up again in her eyes inperceptibly. "Gye Suk, don't tell this to my mother. Or to anybody else,..."

"Why?"

"There's no need to spread the gossip, is there?"

"So you must be still reluctant to give him up. Rubbish! Why can't you hold your peace? What are you so afraid of?"

"Oh, stop making such a fuss."

Ogi didn't like to see Gye Suk chattering.

When she got home, her mother was chopping firewood in the yard. She didn't say a word about meeting Bong Guk, she went silently into the kitchen to prepare supper.

At supper, her mother told her about Bong Guk's visit.

"Today I gave him a good talking-to. I told him to forget that absurd idea and to get on with his work.... I said I would not tolerate if he loafed about out of vanity... I taught him a sound lesson today. I must have shaken him a bit."

"Oh, Mother...."

She had supper, her eyes cast downward.

Bong Guk came back to Kangbuk-ri in anger. After supper

he went over to the co-op farm's management board office, where he was informed that the farm machine station had ordered him to join in the work to level the fields in Kangnam-ri from the next day on.

"Join in the work to level the Kangnam-ri fields? Who said so?"

"Probably the manager", the accountant explained. "A few hours ago our board chairman received a phone call. He said how he could send the tractor there when we were so busy here. But the manager told him to send the tractor to Kangnam-ri for a week whatever happened."

Bong Guk fumed with anger. He felt disgusted even looking towards Kangnam-ri because of Ogi and her mother, and now he had to drive the tractor there to help their work? Infuriated, he went over to the telephone to make a call.

"Hello, is that Comrade Manager? I am Kim Bong Guk in Kangbuk-ri."

"Oh, I rang up a few hours ago. You'll have to work in Kangnam-ri from tomorrow on the field-levelling project."

"I can't."

"Why? What's the matter?"

"I can't go."

"Why can't you go? What are you talking about?"

"We are very busy here on this co-op farm, too."

"I know that. The chairman of the board and I had serious discussions. Don't worry about it, and go to Kangnam-ri early in the morning. Our station should give assistance to the field-levelling at Kangnam-ri. So you go over and work there just for a week."

Dead silence.

"Did you hear me?"

More silence.

"Are you still on the line?"

"I am."

"So you'll go tomorrow for sure?"

No reply.

"Why don't you answer?"

"I'll see, I'll probably go."

"Probably? Say yes or no."

"Yes."

Bong Guk couldn't really say no. He put the receiver down. He could hardly contain his resentment. He sat down on the chair, his face flushed. Then there was another call to make him still angrier. It was from the chairman of the Kangnam-ri co-op farm. He asked if it would be necessary to send some of his farmers to break the ice over the river, so that the tractor would cross next morning. Purple with rage, Bong Guk answered surlily that he would drive to the county town about four kilometres away to cross the bridge.

"Drive to the county town? Why waste petrol and overuse the machine? The field is only a stone's throw from there. Cross the river after the ice has been broken."

"I've got something to do there. There's something wrong with my tractor, and I must drop in at the repair shop. Humph, they keep sticking their noses into everything."

Bong Guk spat out the lie and slammed down the receiver.

The next morning Bong Guk couldn't get out of start for Kangnam-ri. He thought it over again when he woke up. The problem was how to get away with making the detour via the county seat. He couldn't find a convincing excuse to tell the people of his farm machine station if they asked why he had taken the roundabout way and it would weigh on his conscience. But milk was already spilt. He had told the Kangnamri co-op farm chairman that he would drive through the county seat, and nobody would be sent to break the ice. And if he crossed the icebound river alone and the tractor sank in, he would have to break the ice himself. That would be a real mess! If the villagers of Kangnam-ri saw him, they would speak ill of him as a troublemaker. The more he thought about it, the more worried he was.

"Damn it all, they're going to pay for it."

He had been so worried that he had complicated the situation. And yet, he gritted his teeth cursing other people whom he couldn't put his finger on exactly. He decided that there was nothing for it but to go through the county seat and then along the main road by the river with his back to the icy wind. That morning there was a sharp cold after a few days of milder weather. Bong Guk sped up the tractor so as to get to Kangnam-ri as soon as possible, via the county seat. But he was thunderstruck near the ford crossing to Kangnam-ri.

Someone was crossing the wide river towards this side, having already broken most of the ice. Bong Guk scrutinized over the steering wheel to see who it was. It was Ogi of all people. Her legs were in the water and only her upper body dressed in black could be seen above the ice. She was holding an axe and breaking the ice with lightning speed. Bong Guk was frozen to see this unexpected scene, but the sight of Ogi just made it worse.

"Oh, hell... she wants me to cross?"

He drove past the ford. Having driven on some 100 metres, however, he felt sorry for what he had done. He stopped the tractor and stood up in the cab to look across the river. In the cold windstorm Ogi was standing in the ice-broken water, staring at him. She seemed to be wondering why the tractor had driven past. Bong Guk thought that he had gone too far, and he was embarrassed. He drove back to the ford.

Though he returned to cross the river, he became more brazen.

Seeing the tractor come back, she carried on working. She wielded her axe desperately. Glittering ice chips and powder were flying in all directions. Bong Guk drove his tractor onto the ice. But before long the ice crumbled and the machine sank in the water. The wheels skidded, eating into the gravel on the riverbed.

"Wait a minute. I'll break the ice through", shouted Ogi not far from him. Bong Guk would not listen to her and hit the ice repeatedly with the wheels. However hard he tried, it was impossible to break through the ice. Now, he could clearly see Ogi who looked so ghastly. A strong gale blew in frenzy and the water was up to her thighs; gasping, she kept breaking the ice with all her might.

All her clothes were wet and cold water was streaming down from her head, from her face. She looked as if fighting with some cruel enemy. Bong Guk jumped out of the cab and rushed towards her. He slipped his hands into her armpits and lifted her up out of the water.

"Get out of the way!" he thundered, and snatched the axe out of her hand.

"Please don't get yourself wet in this cold weather. Let me finish it."

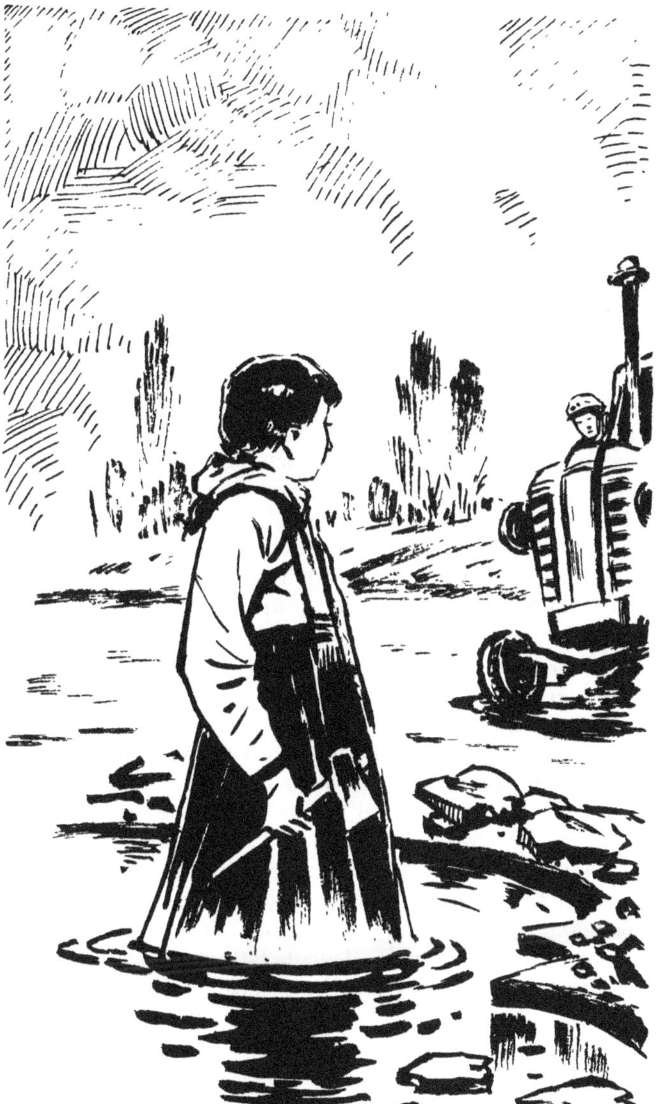

"You don't know how to break the ice. Why can't you do it like this, stepping backwards?"

"I did, but the ice kept on giving in."

"It won't."

Bong Guk drove the axe into the ice, pacing backwards. Soon the ice cracked and he fell into the water with a bump.

"God damn it!" swore Bong Guk. He smashed the ice with a terrific force, standing in the water.

Water was streaming down Ogi's body. There were bits of ice entangled in her hair.

"The farm told you to do this?"

"N-no...."

"Why did you come out here, then? Want to die?"

Ogi was speechless. Only her pale lips were trembling. Last night, Ogi had heard from the team leader that Bong Guk would be coming over with the tractor to help their farm with field-levelling. She had spent a wakeful night, worrying about the ice on the crossing. What if they do not arrange to break the ice, she asked to herself. Regardless of Bong Guk's breaking their engagement she simply didn't want to believe in that. In the morning she hid the axe handle up her sleeve and went out to the river.

On breaking the ice, Bong Guk flung the axe towards Ogi, meaning for her to catch. He had taken the axe from her to break ice in the water, but his anger was not softened. The axe slid on the ice missing her heel by a hair's breadth. Ogi quickly picked the axe and walked away in haste. She was a bit happier, and didn't feel cold. She even had an urge to swim in the water. Reaching the bank, she hid the axe inside her sleeve again, held the blade in her hands, and started to run.

When Bong Guk arrived at the workplace, farmers were gathering in. In the wide valley like a plain, the work had already begun. He thought it would be a simple job levelling the paddy fields. Large quantities of earth had buried the low paddies. So levelling would be easier than digging and removing the earth from the paddies. He drove the tractor up to the place where colours were fluttering vigorously in the wind. As he stopped the tractor, farmers flocked around him.

"Why, Comrade Bong Guk, you've come already?" they

asked. "We thought you were coming through the county town."

"Came here directly because I had no time."

"How did you cross the river? The farm was told you would come through the county town, and we made no arrangements to break the ice..."

Bong Guk hated to answer. The wet trousers made his teeth clatter.

"You crossed the river without breaking the ice?"

"If not, why are my trousers wet?"

"Gosh! We are very sorry."

The farmers ran to the mountain bend and instantly brought bundles of wood. They made a fire and stood him by it. Soon steam rose heavily from Bong Guk's drenched trousers.

Presently, when Bong Guk was starting the engine Ogi's team leader came running with a broad smile.

"Say, Comrade Bong Guk, change your clothes before starting to work. Ogi has brought these here. It looks like she is too shy to hand them to you herself. She was there hesitating to come, so I brought them for her. Put these on."

"My clothes are dry now."

Pushing away the offered clothes, Bong Guk jumped into the cab. He took the wheel and ran the tractor to the place where the earth was being dug.

The site was like a beehive, with oxcarts and wheelbarrows everywhere to carry away the soil. The tractor and trailer did a long shuttle run.

Amid the seething human sea, Bong Guk could not find Ogi for some time. Then a small girl in a pink jacket came in sight. She was shovelling zealously down yonder where there were a string of waiting ox carts.

"I say, Ogi, how happy you are today? Bong Guk is here carrying the earth with his trailer to ease your backbreaking work."

The girls were jabbering bubbling around her, all except Gye Suk who pouted her lips towards Bong Guk more often than not.

"Fiddlededee! I hate to see that sort of trailer. A fool like Ogi might like it...."

The girls didn't yet know why Gye Suk was so irritated. Ogi

alone knew it and was in a fidget lest she should open the wrong side of her mouth.

Ox carts came one after the other. The girls shovelled up the earth all in a sweat. Ogi took off her jacket. At times she would glance at Bong Guk's tractor chugging up yonder. Her heart was enwrapped with something hot like fire. She was anxious to work harder and shovel three times as much as the others today, goodness knows why.

Meanwhile, Bong Guk was in a sullen mood all day. The farmers pleaded with him to go and have lunch with them but he refused, saying that he was not hungry. He was left alone in the workplace with no one else in sight.

He lingered about in a gloomy mood before he spread his fur coat on the grass to lie on it. But he got up again in sheer anger. He felt like a lone dog. He even wondered why he was lying alone on the grass when the farmers had gone home for lunch. This time last year he had ploughed the fields in this village. He was in high spirits then. Now he thought he had taken a wrong road but at that time, right after school, vigour and ambition had been alive in him; the joy of learning while working in the grand reality, the honour of helping the farmers with a machine sent from the Party. Indeed, he had worked with passion. At times, when he was repairing the machine in the field, the farmers would crowd around him to lift him up in token of their gratitude.

These reveries saddened him. He lit a cigarette and puffed slender clouds of smoke into the air. When lunchtime was nearly over he happened to notice Ogi running towards his tractor from yonder. She seemed to have finished lunch already. She looked about for a few seconds and put something in the cab and ran off. It might be a lunch box. The fluttering pink jacket soon disappeared down the slope.

"What an odd girl! The more blows she gets, the braver she becomes. What does that mean?"

Bong Guk mumbled to himself crossly. Then, he stared in the direction where Ogi had gone.

"Do as you like...."

Bong Guk flicked away the cigarette and lay down again. He tightened his lips for a while glaring into the blue sky.

Anger spread again over his face but tears gathered in his eyes in spite of himself.

"That tiny pea is real sour."

Bong Guk wanted to hit Ogi with his fist if she was beside him.

But tears ran from his eyes on account of his compassion for the girl. He thought it unfair that a man can't do a thing the way he intends.

He hated Ogi, but her behaviour was unforgettable and cut into his heart. He had never known that there was such a tremendous thing in her tiny heart. Bong Guk had seen a plum flower blossoming in the snow. The flower was small but it had tenacity of life and an aromatic scent. Bong Guk felt like comparing Ogi to that flower.

But that tiny pea called me vain, he thought disgustfully. Am I vain? She said I don't understand my situation and my honourable work. Hm!

This thought surged up in his heart again.

The afternoon work began. The people worked with greater vigour and animation. Merry laughter was heard here and there. But Bong Guk drove his tractor as sulky as ever.

However, his attitude gradually began to change. The next morning his shoulders drooped and his face was lacklustre. In the breaks he avoided people and smoked alone. He was meditative. This is unbearable, Gye Suk thought to herself. Ogi had said Bong Guk had made an absurd declaration in a fit of fury but in the light of his behaviour, it was now obvious that he is going to break his engagement with Ogi. He might refuse to take the clothes and lunch box from Ogi, but why should he stay at the farm's hostel, completely ignoring Ogi's home? Ogi must be a fool or an idiot. Otherwise, she wouldn't tolerate it. Gye Suk thought Ogi's mother did not know it yet, and she decided to let her mother know the whole thing, so that she would take it out of him. One night Gye Suk visited Ogi's mother at home.

Gye Suk told the mother everything she knew and angrily declared that Ogi was a fool.

Ogi's mother was dumbstruck and shook her head violently. She had scolded Bong Guk during his last visit, but she had never imagined that things would turn out like this. She had simply thought that Bong Guk took lodging at the hostel while working here because she had told him off.

So he stays there now as he intends to disengage, she said to herself. A broken engagement of all things! This was a bolt from the blue—Does he regard the matrimonial affairs as a game?

Ogi's mother was angry with Bong Guk, but still angrier with her daughter.

Why, that hussy dare not protest at his breaking the engagement but takes him the clothes and lunch box, she said to herself. God forgive me! Why did I give birth to such a foolish child! In a frenzy of anger she did not notice Gye Suk leaving.

I mustn't sit here with my arms folded, she resolved. I must go to the rascal's lodging and hear what he has to say. But where on earth is my stupid hussy?

Ogi's mother rose to her feet, her chin trembling. She readjusted her skirt string, went out of the house and walked off quickly.

On her way to the village, she found Gye Suk standing at the roadside.

"Why are you standing here?"

"Hush, Mother. Bong Guk and Ogi have just passed by. Perhaps they are going to decide whether to break up or not."

"Where were they going?"

"Down to the river, I expect. Come along, and let's see if we can overhear what they are talking about."

The heart of Ogi's mother fluttered more and more. Gye Suk's heart was pounding, too, angered over the matter as if it were her own. Stealthily they made for the river.

Bong Guk and Ogi were sitting on the riverbank. Ogi's mother and Gye Suk hid behind a hawthorn at the bottom of the slope.

The voices of the young man and woman wafted on the air.

"Anyway, I take off my hat to you. I never knew you had such a terrible heart. But you still think I'm vain?"

"I do."

"You don't like my going to university to develop?"

"Why shouldn't I? I do like it. But you must take your present situation into account. You've trained as a technician under the care of the state, so how can you desert the farm when mechanization is in full swing? ~~Whatever we do we have to assess it with our conscience—whether or not it will benefit the state.~~ So wouldn't it be better for you to study at the same time as contributing your technical skill to the mechanization of farming, which is so very important? Yesterday I received a reply from my brother in Kim Chaek University of Technology."

"Letter, reply? What about?"

"I wrote to him, you know. I asked him how to apply for the correspondence course and when. The entrance exam will be in summer, he said. And he advised me to tell you to prepare yourself. Of course, I know you have raised your scholastic attainment through homestudy, though you only finished junior middle school. Yet, I beg you to get yourself ready so you don't fail the exam."

Bong Guk did not speak. He looked up blankly at the moon, his shoulders drooping and all his normal bounce gone.

"Did you get all that? Do please change your mind. Please."

Not a word from Bong Guk.

"You can study and still drive the tractor, can't you? Honour satisfied, your duty done. You ought to know the workplace is an excellent school. I am not boasting that my educational level has improved, but I'm going to apply for the state qualification exam for agro-technicians this summer. I've also learnt a lot while working on the farm after finishing junior middle school. I am sure I'll pass in several subjects, if not all of them. Two comrades on our farm passed the exam and are now full-fledged assistant agro-engineers. One of them is very good at soil science. I met him yesterday and asked him to talk to you. You met him?"

"Yes."

"Did he tell you the way he studied while working on the farm?"

"He explained it in great detail."

"You can do just as he did, can't you? As for me, I'll follow his example to attain my goal."

"I see. I think I understand now."

"You agree with me?"

"Certainly. I'm always powerless with you."

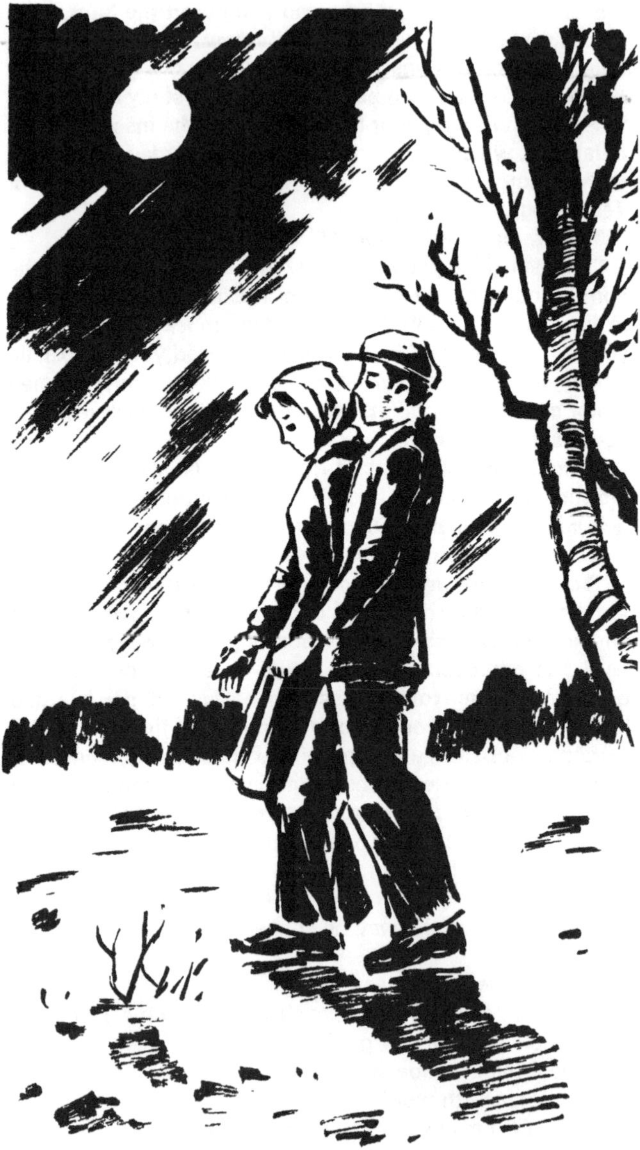

"Oh, please...."

She seemed to be wiping away the tears.

"Look, Gye Suk. She is not a fool after all, is she?" Ogi's mother grasped Gye Suk's hands, deeply impressed. Gye Suk couldn't answer.

"I thought she was a silly hussy, but she has proved awfully strong."

"Mother, I misunderstood Ogi. I really didn't know she is such a girl." Gye Suk whispered, panting. Tears shone in her eyes.

Ogi and Bong Guk stood at the top of the slope. In the pale moonlight, they strolled towards the zelkova tree below arm in arm.

I was so frivolous and mean, Gye Suk scolded herself. She could not rise to her feet. Ogi seemed to be far above her.

"Let's go, Gye Suk."

"Yes."

Gye Suk quickly turned her tearful eyes from Ogi's mother and stood up. Ogi's mother trotted on in high spirits. She had an irresistible impulse to hug her daughter and kiss her pretty cheek.

March 1961

Fellow Travellers

Kim Byong Hun

It all happened last year. I was on my way home from the plenary meeting of the provincial Party committee.

What had been decided at the meeting for our county was no ordinary task; so, before starting on the homeward journey, I put through a long-distance call to the county seat. I wanted an executive meeting of the county Party committee the following morning.

Even in the train I kept going over the decisions taken at the meeting. Then my thoughts turned to the proposals I would lay before the county executive meeting. The task was a hard one for our mountainous county.

After racking my brains for some time a few basic directions and methods began to take shape in my head.

One by one I began to picture the members of the executive body who would be there tomorrow morning, and the tasks each one could undertake. Then, as if they had been facing me, I said:

"Well, what d'you think?"

I could see every face clearly, yet no one gave me a clearcut answer. Yes, everyone looked serious enough—I suppose it reflected the seriousness of the tasks. But they all seemed hesitant; maybe they were thinking that more concrete measures should be taken.

I could not blame them; after all, I myself was thinking along the same lines. There was still a lot to be desired in the plans which I had thought out. I must reconsider the plans more seriously and make sure they were realistic....

Thinking this way, I turned my eyes to look outside.

The train was coming out of a deep valley and rushing across a stretch of open country. The warm June air carried the bitter-sweet smell of the mugwort. And from the loudspeaker in the train came some orchestral music.

"Well, I guess I have to do some more thinking! After all, what our county must do is no mean job.... Maybe, I should just inform them about the decisions and resolutions tomorrow. Perhaps then we can have some discussions on the subject, and I could ask them to give it more thought..."

With these thoughts, I stood up and lit a cigarette.

In the front of the coach a group of passengers were playing with a child, a beautifully dressed child. People were enjoying playing with him. There were a few old men in the seats next to mine. They had a bottle of ginger wine on the little table attached to the window sill. I must say they were in high spirits.

Eventually I went towards the vestibule, where I found several young boys and girls. They were singing some jolly song I didn't know. It must have been a popular song; I could not catch many of the words—only these:

> *Oh, youth! Our happiness!*
> *From the trials and tribulations,*
> *Somehow it grew...*

The strong breeze tousled their hair, but no one seemed to mind. They kept on singing. Youth! Trials and tribulations! What meaningful words they were, I thought to myself. Their song cleared the unpleasant thoughts out of my head and a sense of serenity came over me.

The singing sounded more powerful to the fading sound of the long whistle of the train.

Now we were drawing into a village station.

As soon as the train pulled into the station, the youngsters jumped off and rushed to the volleyball court in the compound. Soon the white ball was flying back and forth over the net. They were again excited this time over the volleyball game.

Then the bell went and the train was just about to move on when suddenly the sound of shouting came from the direction of the station. Naturally everybody looked in that direction.

A young girl with some sort of a can in her right hand and a bag in the other was rushing towards the train. The ticket collector was running after her swinging his punch in the air and yelling:

"I'm telling you, you can't do that!"

The girl gave a quick look over her shoulder and ran still faster. When the ticket collector caught up with her (by now his hand was on her can) she was about ten steps from the train. Abruptly she turned round to face the man. She was short of breath from running. To my surprise, she spoke in a low, gentle voice.

"Why are you making such a fuss? I told you it's all right!" With pleading eyes she looked at the ticket collector. The fresh trim-fitting dress set off the girl's good figure, making her more attractive. Her small, dark canvas-shod feet were poised for running. She wore a blue scarf on her head tied at the back in a knot which, with her rolled plaits, looked rather big.

The girl's full face, her complexion tinged with a little tan, was health itself. The deep-set sparkling eyes, her long brows— everything about her gave a sense of fresh vigour attracting people's attention.

Evidently, the young ticket collector could not look her in the face for long. He dropped his eyes and put down the can he had taken away from her. He had stopped yelling.

"I told you this is not allowed...."

"Please let me go. If I don't go today, all this will die. You shouldn't do everything mechanically!"

"Well, I like that. So I do things mechanically, eh?"

Evidently, to the young man the word "mechanically" went against the grain. The blood rushed to his face.

"If you think following the regulations is being mechanical, that's all right by me! But, the answer is still No. Definitely, No!"

By this time the girl too was agitated.

"You always bring out those rules of yours. There are no such rules."

"No? Why don't you read the regulations up on the board. There is one in the waiting room, too. It says in black and white: "No passenger is allowed to board a train carrying live animals..."

"Well! So...."

The girl was groping for a suitable answer. For a minute or so she was silent, then suddenly she took one step towards her opponent, and said: "I read the regulations. But this is different." Now she was pointing to her can.

"These are not live animals. These are spawn. Do you hear me? If what you say is true, I bet you don't even let people carry eggs into the train. Then how about haddock roe? Aren't they what you call live animals? You know, you really make me laugh!"

Then the girl really laughed. Now it was the young fellow who had to do some thinking before he could answer. He just stood there looking silly.

At the moment the train blew a long whistle. It was ready to start.

Before anybody could do anything, the girl snatched the can from platform and in a flash dashed towards the steps where I was standing. Holding the can with both hands, one on the top and the other under it, she tried to put it carefully in the vestibule. Hurriedly I took it over; and I must confess, I almost fell over. Why? Because it was so heavy. When I put the can on the floor the train slowly began to roll out.

"Now, be careful! You'd better give me the bag, as well."

I took the bag with my left hand, then with the other I lifted the girl onto the step.

The young ticket collector who had followed her a few steps, stopped and said, "How do you like that?"

I found the bag was still in my hand and returned it to her. It was a funny bag; a bicycle pump stuck out at one end, and there was some kind of bottle inside. Now she turned to me with a pleasant smile and thanked me. Then she put down the bag beside the can, stuck her head out of the door and shouted across to where the young man stood:

"I'm awfully sorry, do forgive me!" And she really did look sorry. Yet, she could not hide her pleasure—now all was well. She heaved a sigh of relief! Beads of perspiration were on her nose and neck, which she wiped away with a white handkerchief that she took out of her dress pocket. Whenever the breeze rose a lock of her hair trembled.

The glaring sun must have shown into her eyes for she squinted slightly but kept staring at the clear stream running parallel with the rails. Occasionally she raised her half-open eyes to the high mountains in the distance or to the cloudless sky. She seemed to be enjoying the fresh, cool air.

Before I knew it, I was working hard to try and make her out. First she had made me a fellow conspirator in breaking railway regulations. Then I wondered how all this business of the can of spawn, the pump, and the bag fitted in. I made one wild guess after another. Maybe it is a black marketeer's bag (but there aren't any black marketeers now). Perhaps she is moving... I gave up.

Suddenly she turned round and crouched down by the can, the top of which was covered with a piece of gauze tied on with string.

The girl untied the string and took off the gauze. She kept peeping into the can, and then took a thermometer out of it. A thermometer, mind you! By now I was really puzzled.

She read the thermometer. Evidently, the results pleased her for she smiled. It seemed that everything was under control and she could relax.

I was not the only one who was curious. All the young people who had been around the entrance took a great interest in this girl's tin can. So, when she opened the can everyone wanted to have a look. They almost bumped heads. But all I could see, at least that's what I thought, was water. That was all.

Then I remembered the argument this girl had had with the ticket collector. She said she was carrying spawn. Did she say haddock roe, or something else? But I know what fish eggs look like. Certainly they don't look like water. I could not restrain myself any longer:

"Did you say that was spawn?"

Everyone present looked at her face as if demanding a yes-or-no answer. Suddenly, quite unexpectedly she blushed. Without saying anything she covered the can and tied up the string. Now a tall fellow with a funny haircut, rolled his big eyes and said, "It must be pickled roe!"

"Pickled roe!" exclaimed the girl, raising her eyes to stare at him. Her expression seemed to say, "Don't be ridiculous!" But she lowered her eyes and murmured:

"To tell you the truth, I told the ticket collector a fib. There are 50,000 young carp in the can."

"50,000!"

"What, carp? Don't be stupid!"

Everyone looked surprised, but evidently she disliked what someone said about "kidding," as she stood up and said:

"I'm not joking. I'm serious. There are young carp in the can. They are only three days old. The carp are so tiny that you can hardly see them."

She glanced at everyone as if to say if there was anyone who dared challenge her, let him come forward. Sure enough, everyone stepped towards her, saying: "All right, let me see them!"

It has been said from olden times that travellers would do anything to kill time. So, people asked the girl to show them the fish, but the girl covered the opening of the can with both hands and sat down, embarrassed.

"I'll let you see them. But they are young fish and I cannot show them to everybody. So one should see for the lot of you. How about you, Pa?"

She called me "Pa." Of course, I could be called "Pa." After all I was nearing fifty and was greying at the temples. But still! Yet, I felt I could take no offence at what she called me. And there was no time for that as she untied the can again. Now, crouching beside her I peered into the can as she bade me. But still I could see nothing except liquid, maybe water. And I told her so. She said:

"Now, Pa! You should stand with your back to the sun and

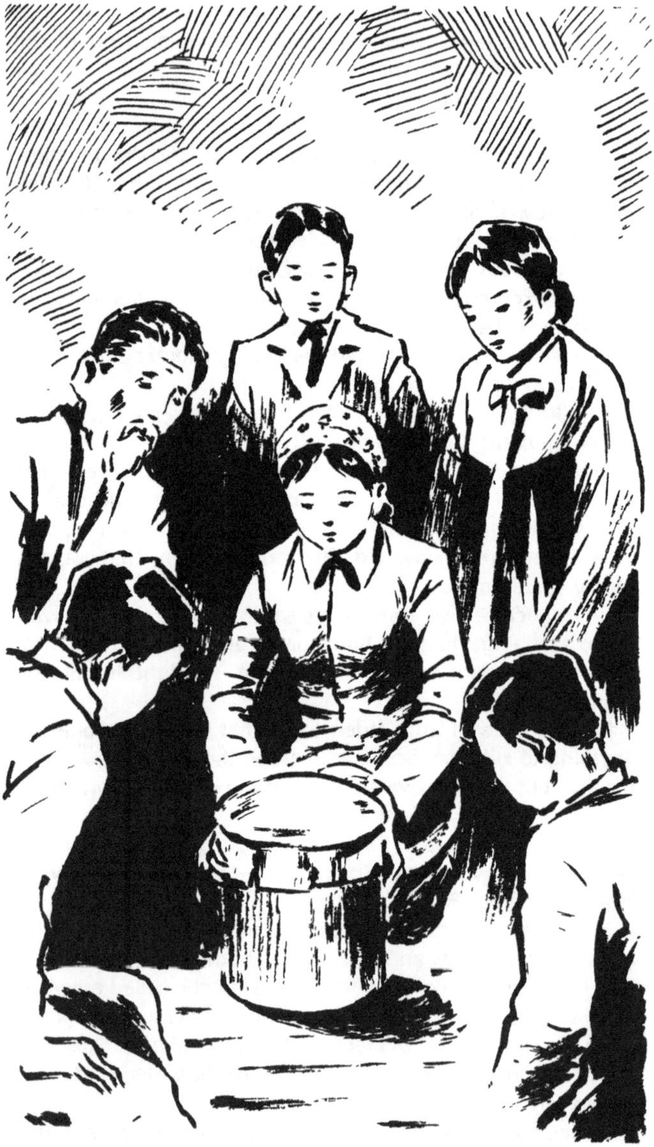

look into the can carefully. Look at one spot. Now you see them, don't you?"

She tried to help me adjust my position saying, "This way, Pa," "No, this way, Pa." Though I did not like the word "Pa," I adjusted my position as she ordered, and, sure enough, I saw something—something so tiny that you could hardly see unless you strained your eyes. And there were a whole mass of them. I exclaimed:

"Yes, Oh so! Now I can see them!"

The girl looked pleased with my discovery. But the husky fellow, the one with a funny haircut, was doubtful. He insisted that he must have a peep.

"What do you know! They're moving alright!"

The man was startled. Now the girl was assured—her face wreathed in smiles, she covered the opening securely.

An elderly looking man—he was one of my neighbours who were having wine—kept looking at the girl with an unlit pipe in his hand. At last he asked the girl:

"Well, young lady! What are you proposing to do with them?"

"We'll raise them, Grandpa!"

"Raise them! You don't say!"

Grandpa was impressed. But the fellow who had seen the fish was more difficult to convince.

"Yeah, but how long will it take them to grow into fish?"

"My! You are certainly impatient, aren't you? When it is young nothing looks like much of anything. Did you ever see a young tiger? It's no bigger than a cat. The fish may look small now, but in two years you'll see. They'll be as big around as your arm!"

"Come, you don't mean that!"

"Of course I mean what I'm saying. In two years a carp will weigh half a kilo, then in three years one kilo. So, do you know how much fish I have here now? Believe it or not, I've some 25 to 50 tons of fish!"

She acted as if she actually had 50 tons of fish then and there. She kept shaking her forefinger vigorously at the can while she spoke. But the tall chap was as skeptical as ever.

He was a hard-boiled one. He said:

"So now I've heard everything. But it just sounds like

building a house on sand."

His remarks really made the girl angry. Her pleasant, excited face paled for a second. Seeing this, the old man interposed.

"Now, now, young fellow, that's enough.... Now, tell me, my girl. How will you rear them? What do you feed them on?"

The old man was obviously very interested in her carp. He elbowed his way to the girl. The angry girl still kept staring at the young chap. Evidently she wanted to say something, but was restraining herself. Then she turned to the old man and answered:

"Grandpa! They can be reared anywhere—reservoir, paddy field, pond or breeding ground. In our country, they can be grown practically everywhere. Then...."

Her anger had disappeared by now, and she was herself again. The colour came back to her cheeks and her eyes shone.

"Another thing about carp breeding is this, Grandpa. It is easy to get food, because they eat almost anything. First of all, they eat tiny things in the water, mosquito larva, and all insects that harm rice. And they eat weeds as well."

"It sounds too good to be true!"

This was from the husky fellow who was craning his neck again from the back. The girl answered, smiling:

"That's right! Besides, their manure is good for the soil, too. But, of course, it is still better, if we give them food, vegetable or animal matter. Any grass, unless it's poisonous, of course is good. Then pupae, earthworms, tadpoles are also good."

She sounded as if she were making a speech to a big crowd, gesturing enthusiastically. Why, we're getting a lecture on carp breeding on the train, I thought.

She even unzipped her bag to take out a large book, you've guessed right it was "Carp Breeding." Thumbing through the pages she held it up for everyone to see. There were pictures showing every phase of carp breeding. Now she was completely carried away. She was no longer so careful with the can. She let everyone have a look.

The old man drinking wine, a man who looked like a peasant and I asked her most questions.

Showing no sign of fatigue she rattled on. Only now and then she took out her handkerchief to wipe her perspiring face. Finally this was her conclusion:

"...Now, may I say this. No one should belittle fish breeding. In our country, most conservatively put, there are at least 200,000 to 300,000 hectares of paddy fields and reservoirs where we can breed fish. And do you know how much fish we could get there? At least 200,000 tons! Please think what it would mean to us. The whole country would overflow with rice and fish. Don't think I'm dreaming. It's a fact. All this is just around the corner."

Her words were assuring and, as I looked at her agitated face and her burning eyes, I was tempted to think nothing was so worthwhile as fish breeding. She almost made me feel that I should become a fish breeder right away!

I am sure I was not alone in this. Grandpa and the middle-aged peasant repeatedly told her that, when they went back to their cooperative farms, they would ask their cooperative chairmen to expand fish breeding. Then they thanked her. The old man told her he would surely urge his cooperative farm to do the same. The girl was so touched.

"Thanks a lot, Grandpa! Please do that!"

"Why thank me? It is I who should thank you!"

Now everyone shook hands with her and went back to their seats. Much more relaxed, the girl watched them go back. Then I said:

"Now, come with me. There is a seat vacant next to me."

"Thanks a lot. But I'm all right. I'd rather be out here. Because the air is fresh here and it is good for my fish. Oh, my! What am I doing?"

I could not understand what had come over her. She opened the can and took out the thermometer again. Her radiant face clouded. Hurriedly she took out the cycle pump out of her bag. Then putting the tube into the can, she began to work the pump. I just stood there watching.

Now I understood. She was giving the fish oxygen. I said to myself this girl has thought of everything. How clever and thoughtful she is!

The girl worked the pump faster and sweat rolled down her neck. I offered to help.

"Give me the pump. And you hold the tube tight."

"Thanks, but I'm alright."

"Give it to me."

I took the pump from her. One could hear bubbling in the can. The air was going in all right. Now the girl seemed to feel better, for she smiled again.

When I finished the pumping I also returned to my seat.

Now the train was in a deep valley again. I took a novel out of my bag, but somehow I didn't seem to settle on the book, and the print seemed to dance before my eyes.

I kept thinking about the girl and fish breeding. I rose to my feet and went out again where she was.

The girl was sitting on a step with a thick book on her lap. But she was not reading—it seemed that her mind was far away.

Somehow I felt sorry for her. I offered to watch the fish for her, so she could go inside and have rest. I squatted down beside her and looked into her eyes. She was completely absorbed in her own thoughts, and did not even realize I was there. But what startled me most was that those dark eyes staring into the distance were clouded with tears. I asked:

"What's wrong? Are you all right?"

Now the surprised girl, quickly brushing away her tears, answered:

"Oh, I'm sorry! Is that you, Pa?"

She even tried to smile but then turned her eyes to the distant sky and followed the rapidly disappearing ranges behind the train.

I stole a glance at the book she was reading. It was a novel. The page number showed that she was nearly at the end. I knew almost immediately what it was all about. I sat down beside her and picked up the book.

Leafing through it, I remarked in a jesting tone.

"My! A girl like you shedding tears over a novel?"

There was no immediate response. She did turn around in the end to face me, but I could see she was still rather shaken.

"But, Pa! Why must Sonbi die, beautiful and wise Sonbi? Why must she? In all her life she knew nothing but misery. Why shouldn't she be happy?"

She was so overcome that her voice trembled.

I wished I could give her an answer, for the girl was pouring out her anger against the class society which crushed a beautiful soul, the heroine, under its savage heel. I looked at her. She was silent, wrapped in her own world again. She spoke again with a deep sigh.

"But, Pa! Isn't it true that everyone in our society is thinking how they can do more for others? Everyone wants to help people to be happy for years and years, a hundred years, two hundred years...."

Her eyes began to sparkle again. She kept talking.

"You know, Pa, I think we take it for granted that people should think that way and act that way. In our society we don't think it unusual." All I could do was agree with her. There was a pause before she carried on.

"I simply can't understand how people can be so cruel to their fellow beings. All those scoundrels think about is how to hurt others."

The blood rushed to her cheeks. Her shining eyes were burning. Her words were so moving, I could find no suitable answer. I said:

"They can hardly be called human beings. We call them wolves...."

I wished I had mastered the art of expressing myself better, but somehow words failed me.

"You're right, Pa! They are beasts. I have seen them. I saw the Americans, the devils, drive people into a cave and close the opening with rocks. They thought it was great sport. They were whooping and laughing all the time. When I think of it even now, I just, just...."

Her anger was so intense words failed her. She clenched her fists. It was some time before she calmed down.

"Do you know, what I think, Pa? I think the bodies of water that we see on the globe are ponds of tears or blood that our ancestors shed for thousands of years. We must make the water flow again. But I don't think it will find an outlet until we revenge them. I think that is the mission of our generation."

Her burning eyes were fixed on me. And I kept nodding in agreement.

We sat there saying little, each lost in his own thoughts.

There was a long whistle; the train must be approaching a station. Before long a signal tower came into sight. Suddenly the girl rose to her feet and went over to the can of fish and took out the thermometer. I asked her:

"Nothing's wrong, I hope! Shall I get the cycle pump?"
"No! I only have to change the water."

She took out a blue notebook from her pocket, then hurriedly looked for something. Presently she put the notebook back in her pocket, and unzipped her bag to take out the bottle. By now, the train was in a station. The girl stood on the lowest step and, hanging on the handrail, kept looking around the station compound. As the train was coming to a stop, she jumped off. But, before she did that, she asked me with a radiant smile.

"Pa, please keep an eye on my fish!"

She went dashing towards the gate. Wondering what she was up to, I stood watching her. Soon the girl, who had gone out of the station, appeared by the gate. She wasn't running now; holding the bottle with both hands, she was taking very cautious steps.

I jumped down on the platform and took the bottle from her. The water was brimming over. She was out of breath from running, and beads of sweat were trickling down her cheeks. And her blouse was soaked with sweat.

Just as we got on the train, the signal sounded. Without taking a moment to cool off she sat down beside the can. Then she tipped the pail to one side and let the water flow out bit by bit. She took out about a bottleful of water.

I was interested in how she went about it. It was good sense for her not to remove the gauze, otherwise she would lose all her carp!

She slowly poured the water into the can, then stirred it gently with her finger. When I asked her why she had to do that, the girl answered: the temperature of the fresh water is different from that in the pail, and the sudden change in the temperature is not good for the fish.

Admiring her business-like way, I again reached for the bottle to help her. And soon I realized I was her assistant, a good one too, I dare say. And it made us good friends. I learned much more about her.

After changing the water at the first station I worked the cycle pump. At the second station she jumped off to get water again—and I waited for her, worrying about her getting back in time.

As we talked I found out that the station where she had an argument with the ticket collector was not her starting point. She had come from Samdung, far beyond Songchon.

She had got the fish at the Samdung fish breeding station the night before and was on the night train changing water and pumping in air. She had arrived in Songchon this morning, where she had to change trains. It was there that she had the "fight" with the ticket collector.

So, she had been riding a night train—busy all night looking after the fish. She had not had a wink of sleep. I was really touched.

Her big dark eyes were as fresh as ever. To me, they were a symbol of youth and enthusiasm. Not a sign of fatigue or weariness.

Her blue notebook contained detailed diagrams of the location of wells or streams at every station! She told me she had "scouted" for them on her way to the breeding pond.

When I reminded her she could have got water easily on the train, she shook her head. No, it wouldn't do, because the water on the train is treated with chemicals, which is not good for fish.

I don't remember how many times we changed the water, but it must have been several times.

But something awful happened.

Before the train pulled into the next station the girl took out the thermometer to check the temperature. She knitted her brows. Ah! That's bad, I said to myself. But what's there to worry about? The next station was the watering station anyway. The girl took out the blue book again. Now her expression was gloomier than ever. This must be very serious, I thought. "What's the matter? We're going to change the water at the next station," I consoled her.

She smiled faintly, almost sadly.

"The well is a bit far from the station. There won't be time. I'm afraid we have to wait until the station after that."

"Oh, is that all? Well then, we can give them some fresh air."

"No, that won't do. The temperature is rising. I was rather short-sighted. I did not think it was such a long ride between these two stations, the road grading is steep, too. I just hope nothing will...."

It seemed she could not finish what she started out to say. I did not know what to do to help her.

Suddenly she cried out, "Pa!" Her eyes spoke of her determination. We were in the station. Even before the train came to a full stop, she jumped off and disappeared, calling over her shoulder, "I'll be back right away!"

I wanted to say something, but she went so fast that I had no chance. Looking at my watch—I even followed the second hand—I waited for the girl to come back.

But, as I feared, she was too late. The conductor gave the signal, and the train began to move again. "Wait!" I shouted. But there was the long whistle. I stepped out on the first step. I thought perhaps I should get off, too. What good would it do? But she was not there. What was I to do?

I was so glad to see her when she appeared at the gate. She ran like an arrow towards the train. But it was too late. The train was picking up speed and it was almost away from the platform. I could see her running after the train. She was holding the bottle filled with water in the right hand. The end of her blue kerchief was flying in the wind. She kept shouting something to me as she ran after the train, but I could not make out what she was saying. I said, "Hurry!" "Hurry up!"

Then everything was over. The girl looked small in the distance, she stood at the end of the platform, with a helpless look watching the speeding train. In the end, I saw her sink to the ground.

"Egad, it's too bad!" I said. I thought of her troubled face, and I felt so bad about the whole thing. But there was a more immediate problem. What was to be done?

By this time all her "students" who heard her lecture on carp breeding were out on the platform. Everyone looked worried. There was her fish!

"Something must be done!" This was the young fellow with a funny haircut. The middle-aged peasant wondered it would not be better if we left the can at the next station for her. The young fellow readily agreed with him.

"That's an idea. When the train gets into the next station, I'll call up the station where the girl is and tell her about the can."

Everyone was looking at me, as if expecting me to say something. "Well, what do you think? Will it be all right?" the old man, my neighbour, asked me. He was so worried that he forgot to puff at his pipe. The light was almost out. Of course, it could be done, I thought. But next minute I remembered how her face had clouded over the fish before she dashed off to get water. I was sure we could not leave the can just like that at the next station. How could we? We had not even changed the water. If we should leave the can as it was, by the time she comes for it, all her fish would be dead. No! that won't do. I shook my head.

Hurriedly I took out the cycle pump. Everybody turned to stare at me. When I explained everything to them, everyone said, "What d'you know!"

I held the hose, and the young chap worked the pump. He was in a lather of sweat. When it was over, we again talked about what we should do.

Well, a decision was reached. It was the consensus of the opinions of all present. Someone should get off at the next station with her can and wait for her. There is a night train. And everybody was sure she would be on it. While waiting for her, of course, the one who got off would have to change the water regularly.

But there was one problem unsolved. Who was going to get off? Everybody said they could. But, who? The young chap? Grandpa? Maybe the farmer?

No, they won't do. I felt I could not leave the fish in their trust. What did they know about the fish in the can? Had they learnt how to look after them from the girl? They didn't know about the thermometer, the cycle pump. And would they know the water should be changed a little at a time? Not more than a gourdful at one time! That's right. I was the one to get off. But what about the meeting that I had called for tomorrow morning?

Before we had decided who should get off, the train was in the station.

Almost instantly I dashed into the train and hurriedly picked up my things. Then, before anyone could argue with me I jumped off the train. Of course, I was holding her fish and bag.

The scheduled meeting worried me, but if I took the night train I would still make it. So I chose to wait for the girl. The train began to move again. Everyone out in the vestibule was waving to me, and calling:

"Look after the fish!"

Picking up the pail of fish I took a few steps towards the exit before I noticed a man hurrying out of the station. He had a red-banded cap on. Probably the stationmaster.

Now the train had begun to pick up speed. Obviously the man was disappointed because, as soon as he saw the train leaving the station, he stopped short and made a gesture with his hand, as if to say "What rotten luck!" Then he noticed me and his eyes fell on the can I was carrying.

"Excuse me, but isn't this the fish pail?"

When I said it was, he told me in one breath he just had a call from the previous station about the fish. She had asked the stationmaster to take the pail off the train as she would be here soon.

I told him how it happened and why I got off the train with the fish. He seemed being relieved.

I rushed to the well outside the station to get a bottleful of water, and changed the water as the girl had done. Then I took out the thermometer and checked the temperature. It read 14 degrees. So far so good, I said to myself. But there were a dozen or so fish floating on the surface which I took out one by one. I confess I felt sick about that.

But then I thought things could have been worse. Carrying the can I went into the waiting-room. I picked a nice spot for the fish—on the bench in the centre of the largest empty room which did not get too much sun. It was cool. I sat myself down beside the can.

Perhaps it was from carrying the fish around, I don't know, but the whole of my back was aching. After all, the girl was right, I told myself, to call me "Pa", and I tried hard to shake off the thought. I took out a pack and lit a cigarette, saying to myself, "Well, you've got to take it, old boy!"

I was the only person in the waiting room.

The ticktock of the clock on the wall was the only sound besides occasional telephone ringing in the office.

The station in the deep mountains was a lonely place. It was a sort of place which made one wonder if the train would ever come. But soon I dismissed the thought with a bitter grin.

I decided I should get mad at the girl—the travelling

companion who "made" me leave my train. Just think. I had to sit in the lonely waiting room some ten hours until the night train! But somehow I could not get mad at her.

On the contrary, when I thought of the girl, a smile came to my lips. I bet she must be hurrying in this hot sun. I can see her perspiring face. How surprised she will be when she finds me... As my thoughts ran along like this, I felt good and a sense of satisfaction came over me.

The clock showed that she had been on her way for about an hour. I worked out that it must be about ten kilometres to this station so it would take her at least two hours. Well, I'd better find same way to amuse myself. I took out the novel that I was reading on the train. But I couldn't concentrate on it. The girl must be running with her small fists clenched so determinedly.

Then the fish caught any eye and suddenly it struck me.

"Perhaps, we could start large-scale fish breeding in my county as well!"

I remembered the question came up sometime ago when we undertook, at the Party's direction, the afforestation and flood control projects. We built no less than a dozen of big and small reservoirs in our county last year and encouraged people to use the reservoirs for fish breeding. And there was still a lot to be attended to.

Yet it was pleasant to see that, in spite of my carelessness, the Party's call found a response in the mind of this girl, rousing her to great enthusiasm. At the same time my conscience pricked me. But it's no use crying over spilt milk.

I wished the girl would come soon, perhaps she could give me a few tips on how to go about it. I would tell her how matters stood. Just think. People dig ponds for fish breeding.

But me? There were reservoirs all this time, but no fish!

Suddenly I heard quick steps outside. And the door was flung open. Imagine it! She dashed in. Since I had not expected her for some time, I was surprised to find her there. But the girl was still more startled. She was short of breath,—I guessed she had run all the way. She stared at me in amazement for a moment, her mouth wide open.

"It... It's you, Pa!"

Yes, she must have run the whole ten kilometres. She was soaked in sweat and covered with dust. And her eyes weren't bright any more. They looked clouded and colourless with worry. At the sight of her face, I felt so sorry for her. But I soon collected myself.

"Why are you standing there like that? You'd better look at the fish..."

With a bound she ran to the can, took off the gauze, and looked long and carefully at the fish. Then she took out the thermometer. With a glance at the mercury, she turned around. Her eyes were sparkling again. They were clear and beautiful like shining dewdrops in the first rays of the morning sun. I thought I'd never seen such beautiful eyes.

The girl took a few steps towards me. In an almost tearful voice she said, "But, Pa!" "But, Pa! You even changed the water for me.... I don't know how to thank...."

She seemed so touched. She could not finish her sentence, and there were tears in her eyes.

"You do look silly! And why the tears?"

I teased her, but the funny thing was I too felt a lump in my throat. Evidently tears are not for grief alone; they can be an expression of joy.

The colour came back to her face. We sat down on a bench.

"But, Pa! I'm so sorry you missed your train on my account. ...Now you'll have to wait till the evening train. I only hope that you're not on urgent business. Oh, what am I saying?"

"Oh, it's all right. There is nothing to worry about."

I tried to change the subject to relieve her of her worries. But I couldn't think of anything to say. In the meantime the girl unpacked her bundle and took out a boiled duck egg. Then she removed the white and crushed the yolk before she sprinkled it into the can. She asked me:

"How far are you going, Pa?"

"I'm going to Kasan."

Kasan? Really? I'm going to Songbong."

Now, it was my turn to be surprised. So, after all, the girl was from the same district as I.

"Which co-op farm are you from?"

"Chongae-ri."

"Really?"

"Which ri are you from, Pa?"

"Me?"

I didn't know what to say. Hurriedly I answered.

"Oh, I live in town."

"Really? If I'm not too inquisitive, may I ask in what office you are working? I'd like to drop in when I'm in town. I must figure out how to express my appreciation...."

"Really there's no need to...."

I tried to gloss it over somehow, but she was rather insistent. If I told her I was chairman of the county Party committee, I knew she would be very embarrassed. But I didn't want to put our friendly relations on a formal basis. Eventually I thought out something.

"Well, I'm with the county people's committee.... By the way, I don't even know your name yet."

"Oh, I'm sorry. I am O Myong Suk."

"O Myong Suk! You don't mind if I call you just Myong Suk. How can a young girl like you manage such a big project all by herself? You're sure you aren't after some big name?"

To my question a dark cloud swept over her face. She just sat there saying nothing for a time. Her face was sober. Her right hand nervously rubbed her knees, her eyes blinking. Suddenly she looked up.

"Perhaps you're right to say that I'm after a big name. There is some heroism in me, I think. Well, so much for that. By the way, Pa, are you on a business trip? I only hope you were not delayed on an urgent trip on my account."

Changing the subject, she once again looked worried. This girl will not feel at ease, I thought, unless I tell her something definite.

"Don't worry! I am on my way home from a vacation. So there is nothing very urgent."

She heaved a sigh of relief. But not for long. She fired another question at me. This time the girl wanted to know where I had been. Mt. Myohyang was the first thing that came to my mind, and I told her I had been to that mountain. I guess Mt. Myohyang had been on my mind because I had wanted to see the scenery there for some time.

"You were there! How wonderful!"

Her eyes bespoke her envy and curiosity. Well, I thought of pictures that I had seen sometime back in a pictorial and I answered in the affirmative. Again in an envious tone she

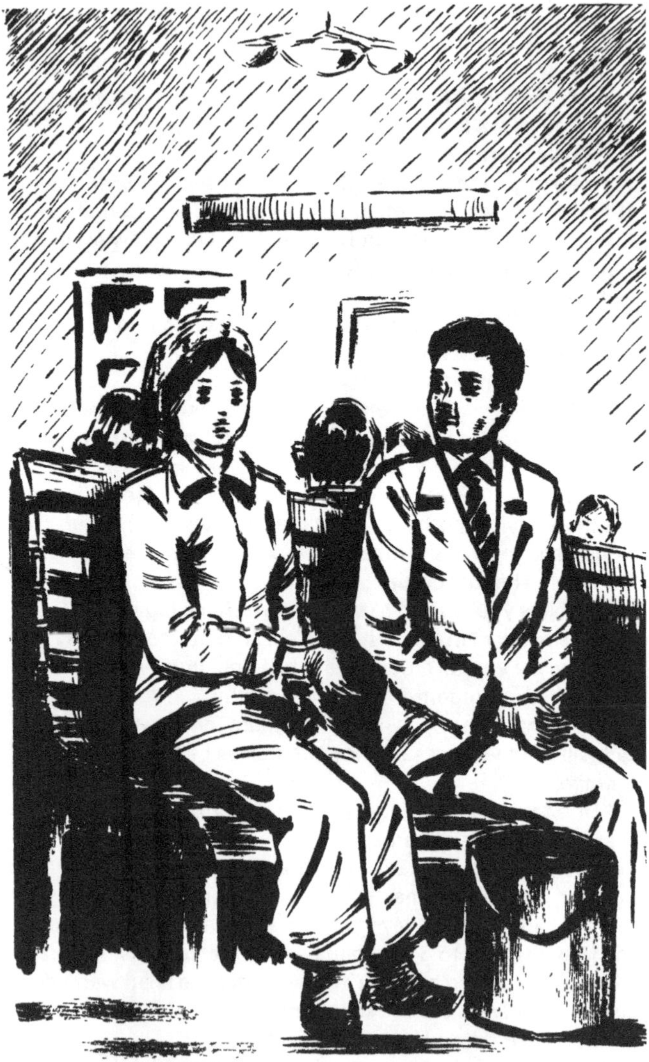

wished that she could see Mt. Myohyang some day. Her eyes narrowed as if she were dreaming.

"Oh, Pa, how wonderful! You know what I wish? I wish, some day I could see every famous place in Korea. All the historic sites, scenic spots, big construction sites, high peaks above the clouds, the boundless East Sea of Korea...."

"What stops you from going? You get a vacation every year, don't you? You can fly all over the place like a bird."

"I like that. I mean when you say 'like a bird.' I think I will do that. But...."

Suddenly her cheerful countenance darkened, casting her eyes at the fish pail in the center of the waiting-room.

"But I can't do that now."

"Why not?"

"Because of that," she said, nodding towards the pail.

I asked her if she was really the only one doing the fish breeding. Myong Suk hung her head and looked at her toes. She was even biting her lower lip. Eventually she mumbled.

"Our management board chairman thinks I am an egg peddler."

"What? What did he mean by that?"

"According to him, there was once an egg peddler who was walking on the ice carrying some eggs. He was busy thinking. He thought that if he sold the eggs he could buy some chickens. Then he would get more eggs. Well, he could carry on with it. In ten years he would make a lot of money. Then he'd have problems about what to do with the money. To buy a big tile-roofed house? Or, a piece of fertile land? While debating it he slipped on the ice and fell with his eggs. They were all smashed, and with them his dreams...."

"Ha, ha! I think he meant to plan work carefully. So, what did you say to him?"

"So I tried to explain everything again and again. Our cooperative farm has many reservoirs, paddy fields, and streams. I told him that if we made good use of all these, we could breed fish. And we would get at least 50 to 60 tons of fish in a few years. And 100 tons in four to five years. Then the chairman told me I was exactly like the egg peddler!"

"But, just the same, he shouldn't say things like that."

I recalled the management chairman of the Chongae-ri Cooperative Farm. He is a determined man, and his farm is doing pretty well. And, to the best of my knowledge, he got along fine with the people, too.... So, I thought he did not take too seriously what this girl had suggested.

"I must confess I did a lot of thinking. I know I was foolish, but I thought perhaps I should call it quits. I regretted that I had stayed with the cooperative farm after I left school. I should have gone on to university."

"I suppose you were an honours student." I asked her, though it was obvious from what she said she was. In fact, I wanted to congratulate her.

"I stayed behind because I had a dream. I wanted to change our mountain village into a home for fish. A year has gone already. But I haven't achieved much.... The management board chairman thinks it is all a whim. And I have often thought I should not have started any of it. Perhaps I am like the egg peddler."

"No, you shouldn't think that."

"Of course, not. But sometimes I can't help thinking that way.... There was a time when I was so downhearted, I went up the back hill and had a good cry. Then I felt better, and thought more."

"Oh! So, what happened, then?"

She was silent for some time. It seemed she was undecided whether to tell me or not. But I was very interested in hearing what she had thought, and she sensed it.

"Pa, you shouldn't laugh at me! There was hardly a soul in my class in senior middle school who wanted to stay behind and work in the village. Some wanted to go to university, some to the factories, to pursue their dreams.

"I was the same at the beginning. Then in my second year, our class had a get-together with Grandpa Pak in the village. We wanted to hear about the landlord from him. You see, a landlord is something that we have never seen.

"I still remember how the Grandpa started. He said: 'Well, my forefathers and your forefathers lived and died in this out-of-the-way village not knowing the taste of rice or fish.' Then he said if there was any one who had a bowl of rice and a small fish, it was the pride of his life. He said the heartless landlord in the deep mountain took away almost everything from the farmers. The farmers worked and turned up the stony fields, turning them into arable land. But the landlord would not leave them even a single potato, so the people simply did not have enough even to make gruel. Grandpa said he himself was a servant to a landlord. One day he got so hungry he began to search for something to eat. He found a few beans in the cow feed. So he picked up the beans and cleaned them. Then he boiled and ate them. He said it had happened thirty years ago. But he said he'd never forget it. As a matter of fact, he wept as he told the story."

There was a little pause. She looked serious and bitter.

"After that get-together we all discarded what we had been thinking. Up to then, we hadn't thought much of our village. It was a village hidden deep in the mountains where there was little hope for young people. But what's it like now? Under the bright sun of Marshal Kim Il Sung something new—yes, something new, is sprouting in our village. Our villagers are raising corn, potatoes, wild fruit, vegetables, and so on for the country. The Party is sending us enough rice—something our forefathers had yearned for but never got! From when I was a kid, I had always dreamed of crossing over those towering ranges that surrounded our village. I wished when I grew up I'd have wings and fly over the ranges to the big, thriving cities or to the giant factories. But this dream of mine had begun to crack. I said to myself, now our leader is doing everything for the people on the roof of Korea so they can live happily. How can sons and daughters of this village say that our place is so remote that it can't be helped if our village is a bit behind the others in becoming a paradise.... One night I made up my mind and jotted down my resolve. I wrote: I will greet the dawn of communism in my village!"

Now the girl was glowing. And how much like mine her dreams were. I, too, following the beacon of the leader, had decided to open the gate to communism for our village and its people, the remotest and most backward of villages. Yes. I was to stand at the forefront with the people in step with the rapidly developing country. This has been my lifelong wish. This has been the task assigned to me, a communist. So what a good travelling companion this girl is!

"You're absolutely right, Myong Suk!"

I wanted to find better words to praise her noble heart, but no eloquent phrases came to me. Myong Suk answered.

"Of course, Pa!"

She went on:

"Then I began to think what I should do for my village. Yes, I thought about it a lot. Then one day the teacher talked about fresh water fish breeding in the biology class. An idea flashed across my mind. Perhaps I should do that. I thought how wonderful it would be, if I grew fish and let the village people have a taste of fresh fish morning and evening.

"I got very excited as I thought about this. I was building castles in the air all day long. I remember very little about what the instructor had said. At any rate, from then on, I began to study fish breeding. In the summer vacation I went up to Samdung to study fish culture for a month....

"I chose to stay in the village and build communism. But even before I could see a socialist paradise, I almost gave up what I started to do. That night I went up the hill behind the house and thought about it all. I felt ashamed. I had shed tears over trifles.... In the end, I got angry at myself and rose to my feet. In the distance I could see the brightly-lit village that seemed happy.

"Yes. I got angry with myself and began to run towards the village with my fists clenched."

The girl hung her head while she spoke. As for me, listening to her I said to myself: that's right. She is not a girl who would throw in the sponge.

"I'm proud of you. Well, what did you do, then?"

"I did something foolish. Instead of presenting the matter through proper channels, I tried to do things all by myself. You know what I did? That night I took a shovel and a pick with me and began to dig a pond. You see, I had marked off a spot by the Chongae stream for the pond. It was my idea to dig a pond and raise fish there.

"Every night, after the day's work, I went out there. I told mother a story: the Democratic Youth League had some special job for me and I had to do it at night. This went on for about two weeks. I got very exhausted. But I was still determined. I was going to make the pond and raise the fish all by myself—not many, perhaps. All I wanted was to have even a few fish and show our chairman what I could do. Then he would think differently of what I had said.

"Then, suddenly, one night a man appeared on the clay dump where I was working. He was the DYL chairman. I think mother went to ask him why I had to go out every night.... Now he pressed me to tell him what I was up to. I didn't want to tell him. But he insisted. In the end, he said I was trying to hide things from the DYL. He had me cornered, I had no alternative but to tell him....

"You know what he said after hearing me? He asked why I had not presented such a wonderful idea to the proper organization. Then he said I was a bit self-important. I don't think I knew exactly what self-importance meant, but one thing was sure. I was foolish and had little trust in the organization.

"After that all DYL members and even the chairman of the ri Party committee came out to support me. Thus, the management board chairman told me I could bring one pail of fish and see how it goes this year. Well, that's the story about this pail. Perhaps, if I make good with the fish this year and show big carps to the cooperative farm chairman next year, he may think differently about the whole thing. Perhaps then, next year, we can use all the reservoirs for fish breeding. Of course it means I am losing a year!"

The girl's long story made me feel as if I was sitting on pins and needles. First of all, I felt Myong Suk should not lose a year in her good work, and something had to be done immediately.

"You should not lose a year. I'll see to it that things are corrected."

"What? Things are corrected?"

Aha! I didn't mean to speak that way. But it seemed Myong Suk did not sense anything special in what I said. In a roundabout way I said, "I'm positive your plans will come through all right. You know what they say: Where there is a will, there is a way!"

"Thanks, Pa!"

"Well, Myong Suk, something just occurred to me. Suppose, our whole county take up your good plan. What would happen?"

"You mean, the whole county?"

The girl was very excited now. Clapping her hands, she rose to her feet, her eyes shining.

"You know, Pa! I have always hoped it would happen."

"Then, why didn't you tell the county people?"

My question seemed to put her down in the dumps. She sank back to her seat.

"What do you mean, Pa? If I can't make even my own village people see my way, how can I make the county people listen to me?"

"That doesn't sound like you. Do you know how many reservoirs there are in our county?"

"I suppose about a dozen or so."

"That's right. There are twelve. The one in your village is the smallest. Now, you tell me. If we use them for fish breeding, how much fish do you think our reservoirs will hold?"

"Every year we can raise hundreds, no, about one thousand tons of fish."

"Then, everyone in the county will have enough fish to eat. Perhaps, we shall be needing a plant to process the fish?"

"A plant?"

"That's right, a cannery. Then, our county, the county on the roof of the country, will send fish to all parts of the country. Just think of it."

"My, my! How wonderful you sound, Pa!"

Now we were talking about how to turn the entire county into a fish breeding ground. I knew the size of almost every reservoir in the county, and Myong Suk figured out that our county would produce about one thousand tons of fish within two or three years. She also thought carps and gibels and a few others would be the best for our county. Then she added that there was no worry about fish food because our county had ample resources. She and I even "decided" which kind of fish would be most suitable to each reservoir. In the end I had a suggestion.

"Myong Suk, I think your cooperative farm should become a sort of mother fish to other villages."

"But, how can our cooperative farm do such a big job?"

"Of course, you can. I think fish breeding will make a very profitable sideline for our people. Of course, you will have to go to some trouble to raise the young ones. But once we put the fish in the pond, we will have plenty of fish in a few years with little effort. Now, we must do this."

"But, Pa, would the county agree to this?" She asked with a dubious look. I had told her I was with the county people's committee. Her expression seemed to say: You sure you can do anything like this?"

"So, you don't put any stakes on what I'm saying. You should not underestimate me like that."

"No, Pa! I did not mean that...."

"Good! I was joking, too. In our country it doesn't matter who makes a proposal. The question is whether that proposal will bring benefit to the people or not. All in all, in our county we haven't done a thing with our reservoirs. So we do not know how much damage we have done to the people."

I talked to her slightly agitated. I was obviously rebuking myself. She stared at me, her eyes wide open.

"Myong Suk, I'll tell you what! When I go back to the county, I'm going to tell the county Party committee everything we discussed today. Then I'm going to ask them to tell your chairman to show more interest in your work. What d'you think of that?"

"County Party organization? Really, you mean it?"

"Of course I do!"

"If that happens, things would be quite different. If my farm were behind me and the whole county starts rolling the ball... Oh, my! How wonderful it would be! Pa, you can do it?"

We again went over what we had discussed and recalculated it all. And I put it all down everything in my memo.

Suddenly there was a voice from the station office.

"Yes, yes, I understand. You mean freight train No. 46. I am to detach two cement cars, right?"

Myong Suk quietly listened to the telephone conversation, then stood up saying that she would be back right away. She disappeared outside.

She must have gone to the office. I could hear her voice, though I could not catch what she was saying. After a while I lit up a cigarette, and strolled over towards the office. Myong Suk was speaking to the elderly-looking stationmaster.

"Please! You've got to help me. Please look at things from

the standpoint of the state After all, rules are made to help us do a better job. If you don't help me, all my fish will die. In the end, if that happens, you will be responsible for that, too."

"Now, now, young lady! So, if I don't let you go, you mean to say the fish breeding work of your cooperative farm will be ruined. Then I shall be responsible for that. Right? I have been a stationmaster all my life, but I've never seen any one as bold soul as you."

"But please, Pa! Let me take the freight. Next fall, you know what I will do? I will bring you a dozen big carps."

"Only a dozen, eh? That won't be enough for me Seems I am helpless. I don't like to be sued for fifty tons of fish, ha, ha, ha...."

"Alright then, Pa! I won't do that."

It seems that a true heart wins everybody over. Before ten minutes passed, a long freight train pulled into the station, on which I too eventually got a seat. Myong Suk and I sat on the steps of the caboose, enjoying the fresh air and talking about our plans. She told me about gibels and other fish that our county will breed. Then I asked her to tell me something about the young people of Chongae-ri.

Myong Suk readily told me about them, one by one.

Tall Pak turned the hand-weeder into a tractor-drawn weeder, Kim built a weather forecast station, he thinks farming should be done scientifically and he gives a weather forecast every morning. Lads were learning to drive the lorries. A girl was successfully breeding pigs. She also added their drama group was preparing a new programme, a young fellow Choe was working on a brand of new high-yielding corn. And after the harvest there will be an excursion to Pyongyang.

I thought her story would never end. But she gave a vivid picture of the Chongae-ri Cooperative Farm brimming with vigor, enthusiasm, and intelligence. I was convinced that the farm was dashing ahead confidently.

When she finished talking she stood up and began to hum, leaning against the railings.

A small clear stream ran along the railway tracks. On the banks there were green bushes of pine and other trees bathed in the sun. As if mindful of their beautiful foliage, the trees cast lovely pictures in the stream.

Absorbed in her thoughts, Myong Suk's eyes followed the changing scenery. The ends of her blue headpiece fluttered in the cool breezes from the river. The bright sunrays embraced her; now she began to sing in a low voice.

Our youth is happy,
Our life worthwhile.
In trials and tribulations
It grew....

As I stood watching her, I wondered how it was possible for a girl of twenty to think and plan so well? How was it possible that this young girl had such a big heart? Just think. There is a girl who did not have a wink of sleep all night, hopping about as gay as a bird and full of energy. She had shed tears, laughed, she had worried about her fish. She had talked and talked. She is vigour itself. I kept asking myself: Where does this girl get all that energy from? With that kind of heart, I am sure, nothing is impossible for anyone. Here is a happy soul! How blessed the land is!

A fresh sense of happiness filled me. Could there be anything happier for one than living in a land where, under the bright sun, the leader, such intelligent, enthusiastic and strong-hearted youngsters as Myong Suk work? How good it is to devote oneself to a better future for a nation of such souls!

I could not suppress a swelling sense of joy. Before I knew it, I was singing with the girl—the tune had become familiar by this time.

Our train pulled into her station, Songbong. I helped her with her things to the exit. Now I had to say good-bye to my friendly fellow traveller, and a reluctance came over me. Suddenly I remembered that it was 32 kilometres from the station to her village, Chongae-ri. I told her I would give a note to the head of the Songbong-ri public security substation. I told her I knew him well enough to ask him to arrange a ride for her.

She thanked me, but said I didn't have to bother about the note. Because, she added, she was expecting the DYL chairman who was to come for the weeder that he had left to be repaired. I noticed her blush as she mentioned the name of the DYL chairman. I should have guessed that, I said to myself.

"That's good," I told her. "I think your DYL chairman is a good fellow."

Now she blushed up to the eyebrow, and I regretted that I embarrassed her.

At that moment the train whistled. With a warm handshake we said good-bye to each other. She kept saying that she would always remember me. As I stepped towards the train, a feeling of remorse gripped me. Of course, I had not meant to deceive her but until the last moment I had kept my identity from her. Well, it was too late now to tell her who I was. I would go and see her one of these days. And when I go up to Chongae-ri, perhaps I can explain everything to her. I was thinking to myself, I must start the fish breeding in Chongae-ri right away. But, who will take charge of it? Of course, it should be Myong Suk. But she is still too young. What of it? She has a big heart! She can do it, I'm sure. I was about to board the train, when there was Myong Suk's voice calling me "Pa!" After some hesitation she said:

"Pa! When you make the proposal to the county Party committee, please don't mention a word about our chairman."

"Why?"

"Because I think our chairman is a very good man. Only he knows very little about fish breeding."

"But you will be losing a year."

"No I won't. I don't think I'm doing enough. I will do everything to make our chairman see things my way. I am sure he will let me bring two more pails of fish. So, please, you just tell them about the county taking up the whole question of fish breeding."

"Are you sure you can do it by yourself?"

"Of course, I can. Well, if I can't make it, I'll come and see you. Perhaps I'll go to see the county Party chairman myself."

"County Party chairman?"

I wanted to tell her she was talking to the county Party chairman, but I didn't.

"That's a good idea. You do that. I think you should present your case to the Party organization. And I think you should tell your chairman how you feel about your village, too. I mean what you told me. I think your chairman needs to be told about it. Perhaps you should ask your DYL chairman to help you too.

And if that fails, then you'd better go up and see the county Party chairman."

Again we said good-bye to each other. Myong Suk got out, carrying the big fish pail and package, then she turned round and waved at me.

I watched her moving lightly with her blue headpiece waving. It seemed I was seeing a most beautiful picture, one that would live in my memory forever. Looking at her disappearing in the distance I thought of a plan.

I will take this up at the executive committee meeting tomorrow morning. We will decide the main points on how to carry out the decisions of the plenary meeting. Then I will make each member go to various cooperative farms. Of course, I will visit Chongae-ri. That's right. Party work isn't what you write on paper. Nor is it what you work out at your desk. We must go and encourage such a heart, the big and warm heart that feels and senses the future of the country—and have a heart-to-heart talk.

At meetings and in books these points are all stressed again and again. But it isn't an easy job by any means to make an idea become one's flesh and blood and one's very nature.

There was the long whistle of my train. With a heavy jerk the giant wheels began to roll carrying me on my way—I was fully prepared and eager for a fresh task.

August 1960

Everyone in Position!

Om Dan Ung

1

Chon Chang Min was standing, deep in thought, silently looking out of the window. He had a way of standing by the window and looking out, thinking for a while, before he picked up work every morning. Probably the manager of the building trust that currently was building an important section of the new metallurgy giant had formed this habit in the army, commanding his regiment in the line of battle.

Outside, the morning sun and the blue sea were shrouded in thick fog. Only the truss of the pig iron mixer as yet without a roof and the blurred silhouette of the angular tower crane could be dimly seen. A shrill whistle sounded somewhere, and an object suddenly sprang into the air. Grey fog was winding round the dark object suspended from the crane. Now slowly the thick steel plate was lowered into the roof, and put into place on the truss with a clang. The sound echoed through the whole site, rattling the office window panes as well.

The manager left the window and, with an irritated air, came over to the desk and sat down in his chair. There were five telephones with light green coiled wires on his desk. He picked up one of the receivers and said, "Give me the chief engineer, please."

Holding the receiver to the ear with one hand, with the other he held a red pencil with which he was tracing the intricate lines on a blueprint spread out on the desk.

No one answered the telephone, and the manager irritably began to rattle the receiver rest when there was a knock at the door. The door was opened and the tall chief engineer walked in.

"I was trying to get you on the phone," said the manager putting down the receiver with a frown. Then even before the chief engineer could sit down, he asked impatiently, "What about the crane?"

The chief engineer remained standing in silence for a while. Even when he sat down, he did not speak immediately. He looked very tired. Finally he said:

"No solution has been found yet. I've reviewed the proposal of the technical department chief, and I think there's no ground for branding it as useless."

"So you mean that it will take four months to move a 25-ton crane 6 km?" the manager growled.

"But surely you remember, don't you, that it took us six months when we first brought it here? Now it's taking much less time...," the chief engineer did not finish the sentence.

The manager sat there head on hand, his thick brows were drawn together and deep furrows on the brow. Silence reigned. Suddenly the telephone shrilled. The call was from the head of the construction bureau. He wanted to know when the assembly of the building for the oxygen furnace would begin. The manager did not know what to say in answer. After a moment's hesitation he said:

"Work will soon begin. Our trouble now is that the winch is too small. We are planning to bring the 25-ton crane here, but it will take time to move. Once that problem is solved, we'll let you know the exact schedule for the work."

After hanging up, the manager took his work cap from the hatrack and pulled it down over his eyes. Then he put on his working clothes. The chief engineer picked up his notebook from the desk and got to his feet.

"I'll make a further study of the problem of the crane," he said to the back of the manager who was putting on the working clothes.

But the manager silently made for the door as if he had heard nothing. Then, he stopped short and said, "You must just think of your own position, of where you're standing. You aren't commanding a platoon or a company, you're chief of staff in charge of a division."

Having said this, the manager descended the stairs quickly, head down and hands thrust into his overall pockets.

The yard in front of the office of the building trust was as usual crowded with people and cars. A reporter of the Broadcasting Committee who had just arrived in a loudspeaker van was running up the stairs leading to the office; a design worker was running across the yard a rolled-up blueprint in hand; material supply workers and newspapermen were going in and out of the office building. Then there were artists—actors and actresses who had come to give performances to encourage the building workers and others who had come to give the workers a helping hand; they were sitting about the yard waiting for their leaders to come out of the office.

At the sight of Chon Chang Min appearing at the porch in a cap and working clothes, the manager's chauffeur lost no time in bringing the car up to the porch.

The manager was on the point of getting into the car when he saw the instructor of the planning department running out of the office with a paper. He looked back over his shoulder one foot in the car, and asked "What's that?"

The instructor had run down in such a hurry that he was out of breath. Chon Chang Min gave a brief glance through the

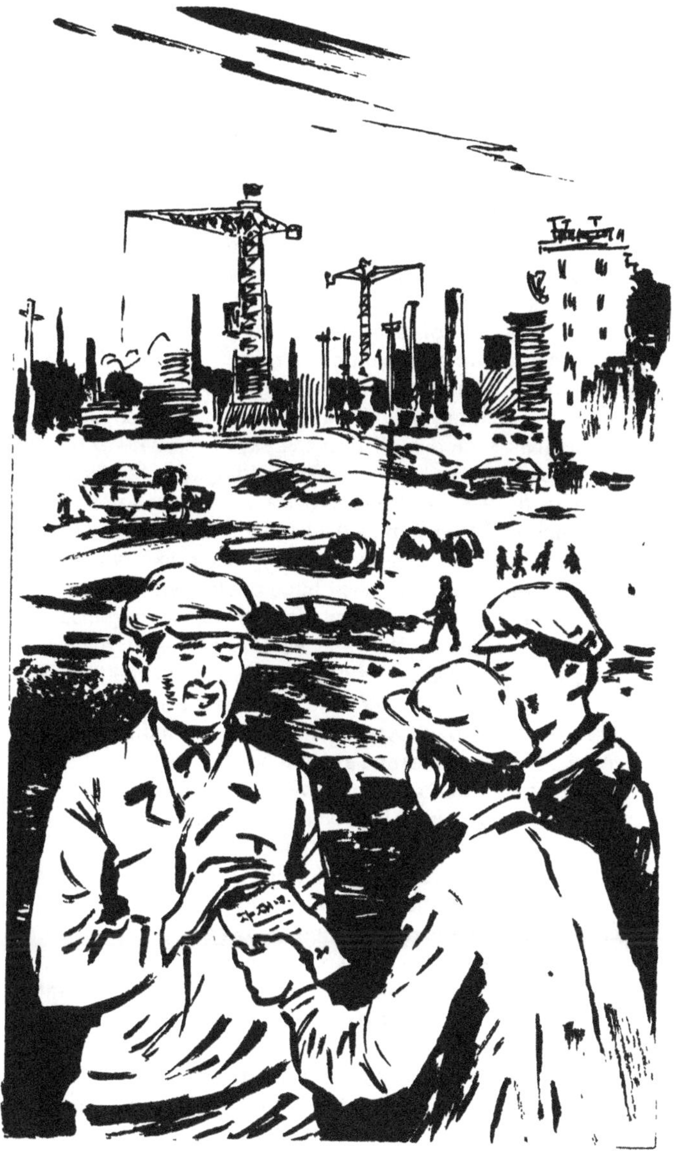

paper, then signed it on his knee and handed it back, and got into the car.

"What time will you be back, Comrade Manager?" asked the instructor. "There are still other papers for your signature."

"Wait till the evening," said the manager slamming the car door.

The instructor stood watching the receding car with a concerned look.

The car sped along a new path laid out on the sandy grounds of the site. Here and there over the sandy grounds steel pillars stood up like huge trees. The car wove its way through the forest of steel pillars and passed by a brown-painted column of a stupendous size.

A newly galvanized pylon dazzling to the eyes under the sun, a new chimney which had never yet seen smoke and tower cranes soared high into the sky Everywhere, bluish electric sparks were flying up from welding rods, and varicolored flags fluttered all over the place. A long string of lorries were running along raising a thick cloud of dust behind them, while excavators and crane cars that looked like tanks with raised gun barrels passed, their huge bodies swaying. An old worker moved off the path, and stood there, welding mask in hand, to make way for the vehicles. Seeing the old man, the manager stopped the car. He got out of his car, took off his cap and greeted the old worker, "How are you, Dad?"

The grey-headed old welder looked puzzled at first, then he recognized the manager and approached him with a smile. The manager knew how to behave towards his seniors.

However busy he was, he would always stop his car and pay his respect to this old welder when he saw him.

The old worker was one of those who rendered great services in restoring the blast furnace right after liberation. He was well past the age of retirement and had many times been advised to retire, but he refused to let go of his welding gun. Even now he would often recount the story that when right after liberation they were having difficulty in welding because they had no proper welding masks and were suffering from eye trouble from overexposure to ultraviolet rays, the great leader Comrade Kim Il Sung had been concerned and had sent them welding masks.

"Well, I've been thinking about coming to see you, Manager," the old man said, looking pleased. "I've something confidential to tell you. But it's hard to find an opportunity."

The old welder squatted down at the roadside and lit a cigarette. Chon Chang Min, embarrassed, stood undecided for a moment before he put his cap back on.

"Excuse me," he said, "but I'm on my way to the sheet metal shop on urgent business. I shall call back later."

After apologizing to the old man over and over, he got into the car. But soon the car had to stop again; about an hour earlier the road that led to the sheet metal shop had been dug up nearly a fathom deep by an excavator for plumbing work. On this big site the ground kept having to be dug up in one place or another, and the aspect changed constantly. Alighting from the car, the manager jumped lightly over the ditch. But it was difficult to walk on the sandy ground—his feet sank ankle deep in the sand. After the sandy ground came the new motor road spread with slag. The manager passed under a high structure which was being built. Welding sparks were falling from the top of the building.

The site was vast, almost endless, and the manager was always pressed with work.

2

The 25-ton crane was a giant. The only things that matched it were the pylon and the dizzily high chimney. Its crest nearly touched the white clouds overhead and the passing flock of wild geese.

When the manager arrived, the crane was working to roof the truss with steel plates. The tower crane was not new to him. But after so many anxieties on account of this crane over the last few days, he looked on it with a new eye.

First of all, Chon Chang Min was awed by the hugeness of the tower crane. Throwing back his head, he stood gazing at its long arm. He was impressed not merely by the colossal size of the 25-ton crane. He was also struck by another of its attributes—its surprisingly easy agility. A young spider-man standing on the roof right opposite was commanding the giant with a whistle and hand signals.

The crane moved forward or backward to the man's hand signals. The crane would swing its arm describing a semicircle in the air before coming to a halt above the truss. It was like a living thing with keen senses, a big tamed animal at the circus watching the hand signals, its ears straining to hear the whistle.

To the manager the spider-man who was commanding the monster by the movement of his fingers appeared a superman with mysterious power.

Now the manager walked over to a worker who was hooking the single-dogs of the wire rope of the crane into the rings on the four corners of the steel plate. Putting a single-dog in a ring, he asked, "Who's the comrade up there, the signaller who's directing the crane?"

"Who? You mean our team leader?" asked back the worker with a freckled face without raising his head. He was busy hooking the steel plate to the single-dogs of the wire rope. When he noticed the manager, he was confused and, putting his safety helmet straight, answered in a military fashion, "He's Comrade Choe Yong Gil."

"What? Is he Choe Yong Gil?"

"Yes, he was assigned to our workteam last fall, straight out of the army."

This was a surprise to the manager. He knew that Choe was a young ex-soldier with only a half year's experience as a spider-man. He had not been aware that the man was a team leader now.

"Is he already a signal team leader?" he asked doubtfully.

"Nobody high up has appointed him team leader," the worker explained with a grin." The girl who operates the crane has the right to choose the signaller, you know. We can say he's a lucky fellow."

In the sheet metal shop each work unit was formed with a spider-man and girl crane operator, and it was the tradition that the girl should choose the spider-man she wanted as her signaller. This was because close teamwork between them was absolutely essential to ensure success in the difficult job of assembling the installations.

A long whistle sounded. The wire rope lying loosely on the ground began to rise slowly and became taut, and the steel plate on which the manager had planted a foot moved with a jerk. Throwing back his head, Chon Chang Min watched the steel plate swinging upward for a little while, and then walked towards the crane.

When he climbed up the iron ladder and opened the door of the operator's cabin, he saw a familiar girl manipulating the control levers. She was rather small built, but looked very steady in her character. For fear of disturbing her, the manager stood still for a while. A steel plate was being hoisted. Only after putting it into place on the roof, the girl rose to her feet and greeted the guest and offered him a stool. But before she could say a word, she had to resume her seat and take hold of the levers; the signaller's whistle had been sounded.

Seated on the stool, Chon Chang Min looked out through the window. From there he could see the spider-man more clearly. With the safety belt around his waist, the young signaller was walking agilely up and down the beams of the roof truss at the dizzily high altitude, giving signals. Watching the spider-man's every action closely, the girl manipulated the levers skilfully according to the signals given by his hand and whistle. The girl's eyes moved as the sensitive indicator of a meter, following the movement of the signaller's hand. As she manipulated the control stick, the crane's long arm swung round in the air, and as the signaller's shrill whistle reached the girl's ears, the crane slowly paid out wire rope or wound it up.

The manager cast his fascinated eyes on the girl as she was operating the machine. Her sparkling eyes were the 25-ton giant's eyes, her well-shaped ears its ears. She was the nerve centre of the gigantic mechanism.

Now Chon Chang Min wondered why he had lost sight of this girl, the nerve centre of the huge machine, over the last few days, preoccupied simply with the height and weight and colossal size of the 25-ton crane.

He had thought just to drop in at the spider-men's workteam to see how they were doing. But now he changed his mind and decided to stay on and discuss the matter of moving the crane with the signaller who, like a magician, had the giant at his beck and call, and the girl who was its nerve centre.

3

A small conference was called in the manager's office at 10 o'clock that evening to discuss moving the crane. On the manager's suggestion, a few spider-men including Choe Yong Gil, the leader of the signal team, were invited as representatives of the sheet metal shop. The manager had instructed that Sun Gum, the girl crane operator, should attend the meeting, but he was disappointed to find her absent because she had not yet been relieved from her shift. In the day he had stayed on the site, had talked over the question seriously with the workers while he helped them in their work and even lunched with them. He had not hit on good idea yet, but one thing was clear. It was his firm belief that, given the agreed completion date and the workers' high morale, it was not possible to take months to move the crane. If the workers' efforts were pooled effectively, the time could obviously be reduced. So for a start a proposal from the technical department chief based on suggestions from the technicians was tabled. The idea was to take off the arm and to take the main body apart into three pieces for the move. That would cut the time to two months.

Compared with the first proposal which, it was estimated, would take four months at least to shift the crane, this was a great improvement. The chief engineer supported the new proposal which combined bold innovation and scientific calculation.

Chon Chang Min himself had nothing to complain about the rational new idea. But there was no time to lose in the struggle for the assembly of the new structure. So he was still dissatisfied with two months' wait.

The room was full of tobacco smoke. The manager stood up from his seat and opened a window to let some fresh air in. At this moment Choe Yong Gil, the signal team leader, rose to his feet.

"We're on a forced march now to the goal of steel production," he said. "The crane could be compared to the gun in the army. If it takes us two months to move a crane, how can we hope to win a battle? So I'm against the proposal."

The manager nodded his head. The technical department head raised his eyes to the face of the spider-man with deep interest.

But the chief engineer was gazing sullenly at the unruly forelocks of the young man. However, he was wise enough to keep calm and to speak affably.

"Right you are," he said with a smile. "But first you must produce a better plan to justify your idea. That's what we want to hear. If you have your proposal, let's talk it over here."

With this he glanced round the people as if to solicit for their approval.

The signaller remained standing, gripping the back of the chair before him with both hands to check his excitement.

"After Comrade Manager visited us a few hours ago," he resumed, "we sat down together and talked over the matter to find a solution. Our idea is to carry the crane whole on board lorries without taking it apart."

"Carry it whole?"

"Yes!"

"By lorries?"

"That's right."

The technicians were not the only people who were taken aback. The manager himself couldn't believe his ears. The young spider-man went on with his argument confidently.

"Of course, we have no lorries big enough to carry a 25-ton crane yet. But if we made a 'raft' of lorries, much like making a raft with logs, I think we should be able to carry even bigger loads."

A stir went through the people present.

"You propose making a 'raft' of lorries?" the manager asked.

"Yes. As you know, Comrade Manager, the sappers line up pontoons across a river and lay planks over them for tanks and artillery to pass, don't they? Likewise, we can build a 'pontoon bridge' with 60-ton traction lorries to carry the crane. That's my idea."

The manager nodded his head in admiration. But he asked doubtingly:

"Well, admitting that we can manage to carry it that way, will such a gigantic crane stand erect and not fall over when the lorries move?"

The manager looked across at the young man with questioning eyes, winking slyly.

"About that, too, I've done some thinking. I believe that the 25-ton crane could be supported on both flanks by the arms of small lorry-mounted cranes. Just as a newly planted tree is supported by props, the giant can be supported by the arms of small cranes mounted on the lorries running alongside."

"Have you any idea what the 6 km of road to be covered by the crane is like?" demanded the chief engineer who had been sitting silent. His voice was calm, but in it there was a touch of the elder's reproach against the recklessness of the young.

"Of course, I know well the rugged state of the road. But our situation does not allow a moment's delay, and how can we make the road and lay sleepers and rails leisurely? Bulldozers should level the ground for the progressing crane. If the bulldozers smooth the road just as sappers open the path for vehicles, and the crane follows in their wake, I think one day will be enough instead of two months."

A hush fell over the office. No one stirred or uttered a word. The manager and chief engineer and all attending the meeting were dumb struck at this bold, original suggestion. Soon an engineer from the technical department broke the silence.

Quoting figures from his memo about the dynamic equilibrium of the 25-ton crane in a state of movement, he pointed out the unsoundness of the proposal.

"Let me explain it in easier terms to convince this comrade...," began the chief engineer. He stood his ivory cigarette holder on the match box and explained the law of inertia and the changing process of the moment of the centre of gravity of a moving object in an intelligible way.

When the chief engineer wound up, the technical department head stood up. He had been sitting quiet till then. He said:

"The idea of moving a 25-ton crane as it is without taking it apart is interesting. Apart from technical calculation, I like the daring of the spider-men. How about tackling the matter with boldness, that is, taking the bull by the horns? Leave the difficult technical matter to us: We, the technical department, will cope with it in cooperation with the spider-men."

The people present began to stir. The tide of opinion which had been inclining towards the chief engineer changed suddenly.

Thus, the meeting ended without reaching an agreement. The attendants were unable to decide between the chief engineer's argument against the reckless spider-men's proposal and the suggestion of the technical department head who refuted that argument.

4

The meeting was over, but the manager Chon Chang Min was still excited. Folding his hands behind his back, he paced to and fro in the empty office.

"So they mean to carry it by means of vehicles? Just as we used to carry tanks across rivulets through a bulky pontoon bridge?" Suddenly he recalled that in those grim days of the war his regiment had smashed the enemy mercilessly from the top of a hill by the 76 mm regimental guns they had succeeded in bringing up without dismantling them, on the Supreme Commander's order to increase the availability of guns.

Didn't I creep up the steep slope of the hill, he thought, with my artillery men, carrying the gun muzzles on my shoulders with regimental commander's shoulder-straps? Gun and crane are two different things; and the circumstances are different, too, but what fundamental difference is there between them? If I make up my mind to hold the 25-ton crane on my shoulders with the same spirit and energy as I had then, in order to carry out the teachings of the leader, what would be left undone? Now, what matters is the law of inertia, or the so-called central moment, isn't it?

The manager kept walking up and down the room; he could not sit still even for a moment.

He heard a knock at the door. He stopped.

"May I come in?"

There was a girl's tender voice and the door opened softly. The crane operator Sun Gum came in. The manager walked towards her, delighted.

"You've come now? Take a seat. Come in and sit down." He placed a chair in front of Sun Gum. But the girl wouldn't sit down and looked straight into his face.

"Comrade Manager, I came across Comrade Choe Yong Gil on my way here. Do you know what he said about you?"

Chon Chang Min bent over and stared curiously at her blinking eyes.

"Well, what did Yong Gil say?"

Sun Gum looked embarrassed and lowered her head.

"He said he had thought you were an audacious man because you served in the army, but, in fact, you are faint-hearted and irresolute."

"What? Faint-hearted and irresolute? Ha, ha, ha...."

The manager burst into delighted laughter.

"Then, why did you put off the discussion of the crane problem at the staff meeting?"

"Why did I put off the discussion?"

Smiling as before, he stalked slowly here and there in the room, his hands behind his back. He was very happy to have a chat with this crane operator who reminded him of his own spoilt daughter.

"There are good reasons, you know? 'The central physical moment of force' or the 'law of inertia' bars my way. That damned 'central moment'...."

The girl gave a broad smile, her eyes twinkling.

"I was told that by Comrade Yong Gil. The opponents of our views know nothing but laws of physics. They don't know the essence of the Juche idea that man is the master of laws. That's why they are taken prisoners of the 'central moment'. And they are underrating our ability."

The manager, seating himself on the chair in a cheerful mood, produced a cigarette, stuck it into a holder and put it between his lips

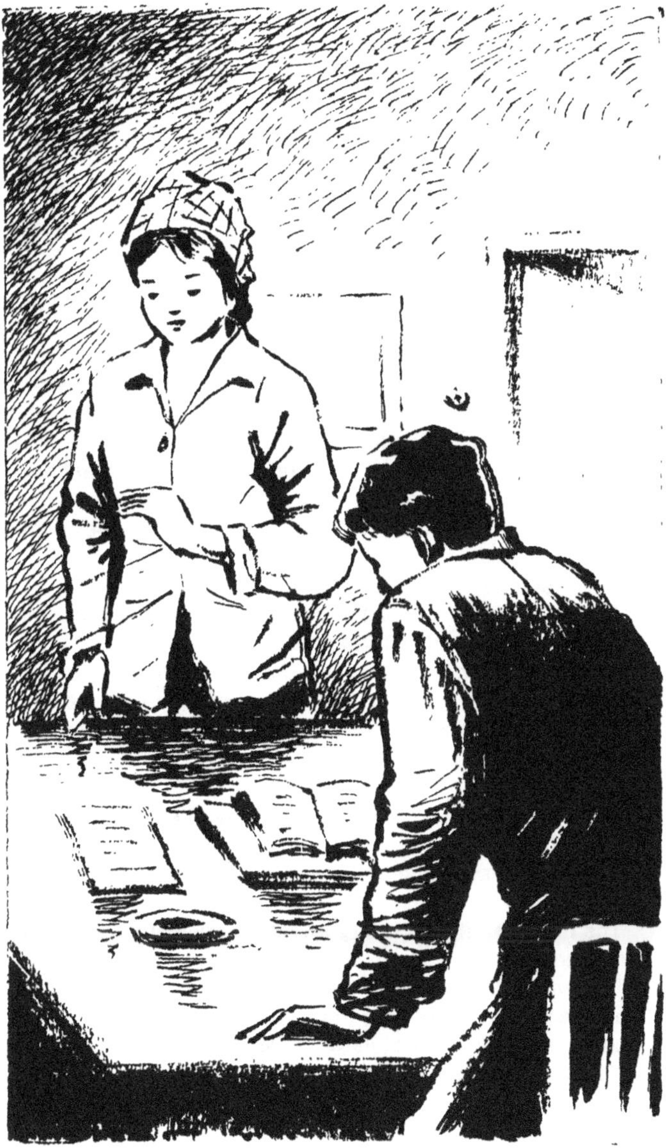

"So you mean the 'prisoners' have no respect for you, eh?"

"Comrade Manager, do believe us, please. We will carry the 25-ton crane over to the very spot designated by the Party without unscrewing a nut on it in a day instead of in two months."

"Have you got any means?"

"Yes, Comrade Manager. We are going to use the squirrel principle."

"What? The squirrel principle?"

"Yes."

The girl laughed, holding the back of her hand over her lips to conceal her smile.

"Comrade Manager, haven't you heard that the squirrel regulates the central moment of its body with its long tail?"

Chon Chang Min took his cigarette holder out of his mouth and looked at the girl with interest.

"The squirrel is able to go up and down slender branches because it can balance its body with its long tail. In another word, the squirrel controls the central moment of its body with its tail."

"Oh, yes!"

Absorbed in her words, the manager rubbed the cigarette out in the ash tray in spite of himself.

"You see, Comrade Manager." The girl took a step forward towards him. "We are going to make use of the arm of the 25-ton crane without dismantling it. Just as the squirrel uses its tail."

"Exactly!"

The manager sprang to his feet, slapping the surface of the desk with his hand.

"Right. You mean like this. Just as acrobats dance on the tight rope. ..."

The manager imitated the movement, spreading out both arms and swaying his body right and left. His heart throbbed wildly with a thrilling idea that it would be now possible to load the 25-ton crane on a truck and carry it intact. But the next moment he felt ill at ease. "What if. ... Oh, no, no."

The manager shook his head gravely.

"Comrade Manager, we're equal to the task. I will take the responsibility."

"No, you can't. I won't allow you to. I cannot let our dear comrades go up such a risky crane." The girl operator took another step closer to the manager.

"Don't worry, Comrade Manager. I definitely can do it. The crane is just like my body. I can manipulate the arm of the machine as freely as I do my arms. How can we hesitate and waver and back down in the face of difficulties when we are carrying out our respected leader's instructions. Comrade Manager, didn't you declare yourself, at the first meeting launching our work here, that our road towards the implementation of the leader's orders is a glorious road?"

The manager's eyes blurred suddenly and he turned round to face the window. He saw welding sparks sputtering all over in the dark. The rain of sparks gradually formed a huge mass of fire before it faded. He fancied he saw the signalman climbing up and down the truss to steer the crane; the twinkling eyes of the girl who kept watching every movement of the spider-man from the cabin, holding the handle in her hands. Why have I failed to recognize these good comrades among my people? the manager thought to himself. Didn't the respected leader advise us officials repeatedly to always work amidst the masses?

Now he remembered that this morning he had told the chief engineer to hold his own position as a commander. Then he asked himself: Where have I stood as a commander? Have I been acting like the officers of the Anti-Japanese Guerrilla Army used to—leading their men in attack and bringing up the rear on difficult retreats? And during the march carrying rifles and knapsacks for their exhausted men or supporting them to keep walking? ...

Chon Chang Min was ashamed. He was conscience-stricken.

Chon Chang Min had always thought he knew his working people well; he had believed that he shared their joys and sorrows. But he now saw that he had failed to recognize the masters of the site such as Sun Gum and that he simply flitted past them like the wind. This morning he had hurried past an old welder who called him on the lane in the compound. He had always been like this instead of going out among the workers to listen to what they might say.

I must build up my position among my men the way the anti-

Japanese guerrilla commanders did, he thought. I must get back into the same situation I was in when I joined the soldiers of the battery and crawled up the cliff, putting my shoulders to the muzzles of the 76 mm regimental guns!

Chon Chang Min spun round.

"Comrade Han Sun Gum! Go back and have a good rest tonight. So that you can guarantee the forced march we are going to make. Let us carry the 25-ton crane intact as you propose. To do that, we will have to get everything ready tomorrow."

Sun Gum's face was full of deep emotion.

"I understand, Comrade Manager."

As soon as she came out of the office, the girl ran downstairs.

The manager remained still with a smile around his tear-filled eyes till the echo of her nimble steps had died away.

5

By nightfall the preparations were over. From daybreak the manager had been so busy supervising the loading of the crane that he had not even stopped for a smoke. The spidermen from the sheet metal shop had taken charge and everybody else on the site came out to help. The technicians headed by the chief engineer were busy giving technical advice. At last they succeeded in loading the 25-ton crane on a wheeled raft made up of three 60-ton tractors. The iron arms of four small crane cars which had been waiting propped up both the sides of the mother crane rising high into the sky.

In front of the tractors stood two roller cars, with three heavy-duty bulldozers lined up ahead and some command cars stood in front of and behind all these machines.

It looked rather like a mechanized corps lined up for the attack waiting for an order to go into action.

As the moment to start drew near Chon Chang Min's heart throbbed with anxiety and excitement. He would look up at the top of the crane or tap the rubber wheel of one of the tractors with his toe.

Before departure the manager called together all the people involved in the march to check that they were all prepared. After reminding them of details of precautions in the march, he commanded in army style for the first time in many years.

"Everyone in position!"

The marchers took the first step vigorously and dispersed to their respective positions.

The Anti-Japanese Guerrilla March rang out on the loudspeaker of the mobile radio van, stirring the hearts of all the marchers.

All the engines were switched on and buzzing, waiting for the imminent order to start.

The news that the 25-ton crane would be carried by lorries had already spread across the whole site, and large crowds were flocking to the scene.

The manager made a final inspection, then walked towards the 25-ton crane.

A car drove up at high speed and pulled up beside him. It was the manager's car which always followed him. The chauffeur jumped out quickly not to be late, and waited for the manager to get on. However, Chon Chang Min walked past, saying to the driver as he went:

"Leave the car in the parking lot. I'm going with these people. My position is over there."

The manager pointed his finger to the cab of the 25-ton crane. On his way to the crane, he came across the chief engineer who was giving work instructions to a group of technicians in an excited voice, staring up at the cab of the crane. The chief engineer's face looked haggard in the setting sun. Chon Chang Min smiled and said:

"Comrade Chief Engineer! Our respected leader has earnestly advised us officials to go always among our workers just as the anti-Japanese guerrilla commanders did. We commanders must stand by our fighting soldiers, must be in the trenches with them in the hardest times. And we have strayed too far away from them."

Chon Chang Min, mounting the metal ladder of the crane, stopped and shouted out at the chief engineer.

"Comrade Chief Engineer, go in front with the bulldozers in

the lead, open up a new road. It's high time we got started. Make haste and take up your position."

On the top of one of the command cars, in full view of the crane cab was the young spider-man Choe Yong Gil as signalman, waiting flags in hand for starting time.

The instant Chon Chang Min himself appeared in the cab, Sun Gum who had been grasping the handle in a strained posture, got up in surprise.

"Sit down, Sun Gum, sit down. I have to be here with you today."

"What?" Sun Gum was perplexed for a few moments before her face betrayed the waves of emotion surging up in her heart.

Sun Gum's hands grasping the handle trembled slightly.

"Are you all ready?"

"Yes, Comrade Manager."

"Then, let's start."

As soon as the signalman waved the flag, the engine revved up and the body of the wheeled raft trembled.

"Forward!"

At the manager's confident shout of command the wheeled raft loaded with the massive crane moved forward heavily. Loud hurrah thundered across the whole site.

Sun Gum's firm hands moved the handle very nimbly.

The manager opened the door and got out onto the tower. Overhead the arm of the crane was adjusting the "central moment" of the huge body as freely as the tail of the squirrel.

The bulldozers moved powerfully and opened a new road through the trackless field cutting the ground evenly with their blades as if to sweep away everything obsolete still standing in this land. The roller cars followed, ramming the ground. The lined-up tractors went ahead slowly but steadily like a column of tanks charging towards an enemy position, stamping the marks of huge rubber wheels on the untrodden road. The deafening sound of the engines filled the air over the field, and the earth shook under their weight.

"Aren't you afraid, Sun Gum?"

Chon Chang Min spoke to the girl operator who was moving the handle dexterously.

"No, I am not, Comrade Manager. I feel at ease because you are at my side."

Sun Gum glanced at him with her moist eyes. As dusk set in, several searchlights illumined their way brightly. A lot of vehicles belonging to the construction site joined in, shedding their headlights.

Each passing vehicle stopped for a while using its headlights to help the operation before they moved on again. From afar it looked like a big lighted city on the move. On the ground and up in the air countless welding sparks spluttered in the darkness. The impressive march with the 25-ton crane moved on through the dazzling confetti towards the target of steel production set by the leader.

1974

Unfinished Sculpture

Ko Byong Sam

May. A woman medical student in a white doctor's coat was walking down the night street of Kwangju (the capital of the south Korean province of South Cholla).

Silence. Blood. Red blood. The roadside pebbles, smashed roof tiles, broken street trees, downtrodden flower beds, open school bags, the pages of textbooks and notebooks fluttering in the wind, children's shoes, smashed buses and barricades. ... Everything stained with blood. This night the white-robed girl was wandering in search of her lover, on the asphalt road splashed with young people's blood, instead of flower petals or spring rain.

The night was advanced in the city where for days an unprecedented confrontation had continued between the townsfolk who had risen up for liberty and soldiers armed to the teeth. Oppressive silence prevailed. She called his name but there was no reply The voices asking for drinking water had gone silent. All the windows were dark. There wasn't a soul in sight in the street.

"Surrender, surrender...."

"Surrender. Then you'll be saved."

The helicopters which had scattered handbills and shouted hoarse at the 800,000 people, had gone, so had the fiends who had till a little while ago created havoc as they shot and stabbed and hanged people right and left. Now, only a searchlight from the outskirts of the city lapped the blood-stained road and gleamed like the eye of a stray cat. The city, in the hands of the uprising, had just been surrounded by the paratroopers rushed here by planes from Seoul.

The girl's face, caught in the beam of the searchlight, disappeared again as if into the ground.

After a little while she shot out of the underpass, uttering a cry and stepped back, protecting her face with her hand from the powerful beam of light. Her graceful figure in the white coat was in sharp contrast to the bleak night. The Red Cross on her white cap was conspicuous as if engraved in her forehead. Her black hair flowing over her shoulders brushed past the green leaves of the trees lining the street.

She was walking down towards Kumnam Road where the searchlight swivelled restlessly. It seemed that the only live moving things in this street were her eyes which anxiously searched the ground and looked scornfully at the sky.

The medical student sensed something strange, which was neither the scent of May nor the air of spring. She cocked her ears and watched a flower bed and beneath a street tree, with the same expression as when she was checking a patient's heartbeat with her stethoscope.

She heard no sound. Not long ago groups of medics had moved about on this street carrying stretchers, and the girl felt as if she was hearing the breaths of the sons and daughters of Kwangju. Whenever she had this feeling, her heart beat as wildly as when she had confessed her first love.

"Hye Gyong.... So Hye Gyong...."

She felt as if she could hear someone calling her, and once she stopped walking, her feet were glued to the ground. Sometimes, she stepped backward and moved forward again and knelt down to feel with her trembling hand. At long last she found a pair of eyes which had not lost their light.

Why, such a striking resemblance! she exclaimed to herself. The pair of eyes looked like those of the one whom she was looking for. They resembled his eyes as she had seen them before he was her lover, before her sexual consciousness had budded. Hye Gyong suddenly looked like a little child and pressed her face against a boy's chest to catch the sound of breathing. The boy's face could be clearly seen in the searchlight. He was lying on his back with a small stone in his clenched hand. His eyes looking into the night sky were so clear and looked like moving and a smile hovered around his lips.

He is still alive, she said to herself.

Hye Gyong lifted the boy, covering him with the skirts of her white coat and walked towards a street tree, calling out hastily:

"Is there anybody in the street? Oh, goodness! Mr. Yong Gol... where are you? Mr. O Yong Gol. ..."

In spite of herself, she winced as she uttered the name of the man she had been looking for so desperately. She stopped and watched the far side of the street. The searchlight passed momentarily to reveal a dark robe moving quietly under a tree. A Catholic priest in a black cassock and cowl was watching the now tranquil street of resistance, which looked as grim as if a storm had just passed over it, mumbling prayers. He had apparently heard the girl's voice, for he crossed the street, his gray hair flowing out of the cowl.

Hye Gyong entreated in a trembling voice:

"Father, I'm student at the Medical College of Seoul University. I came here yesterday and helped to treat the wounded at the Charity Hospital of Dr. An, the surgeon. I came out into the street. I must take this boy to the hospital, but it's too far. If there is a hospital nearby which you know, please help me to carry him there."

The priest held the boy in his arms without a word and walked a few steps pressing his ear against the boy's chest, before he stood still and then laid him down on a flower bed with great care. He rose to his feet, crossing himself.

"You've taken unnecessary trouble, my dear. He has already stopped breathing. There are so many children like him. If we lay him here, it will be easy for his parents to find him."

"Oh, no, Father, he is alive. Look at his eyes and clenched fist. He is alive. Alive!"

"The young soul is too pure-hearted to close his eyes. So he may look alive...."

The priest sank into sad silence, looking up at the starry sky. Hye Gyong checked that the boy's heart had stopped beating, but she would not leave the spot.

The dead boy's future might be likened to an ocean or the vast sky. He would have had to live on to arrive at the highest eminence of life, but he had left his life unfinished. And his seemed to be the heroic death of a giant.

The smile still played around his lips and seemed to whisper, "Sister, I have lived this way for the sake of freedom."

The priest urged Hye Gyong to move on and she followed him without knowing where she was going.

"I thought you were calling somebody just now. Who is it?" asked the priest.

But the girl did not say a word, only looking at the fluttering skirts of the man's black cassock, suspiciously and ruefully.

"You said you were a medical student at Seoul University. How come you are here?"

"This is my hometown. I was born and bred here." Hye Gyong's voice contained the pride and sorrow of a daughter of this city.

The priest asked her whose daughter she was. Her father was already dead and her widowed mother was teacher of the Mudungsan primary school. As she mentioned her mother's name the priest nodded his head.

"So you are the daughter of Mrs. Kim Yong Sun!"

Hye Gyong asked him how he knew her mother. The priest replied that her mother was a most popular teacher in this part of the country.

"Then, Father, I wonder if you know Mr. O Yong Gol. He is not yet famous, but he is a young, talented sculptor." Hye Gyong expected an affirmative reply, but the priest shook his head. He did remember the names of the artists who left world-famous classics like Mona Lisa, but he had never heard of a sculptor called O Yong Gol.

"Don't you know him, Father?"

The beam of the searchlight flashed past her eyes. Of late,

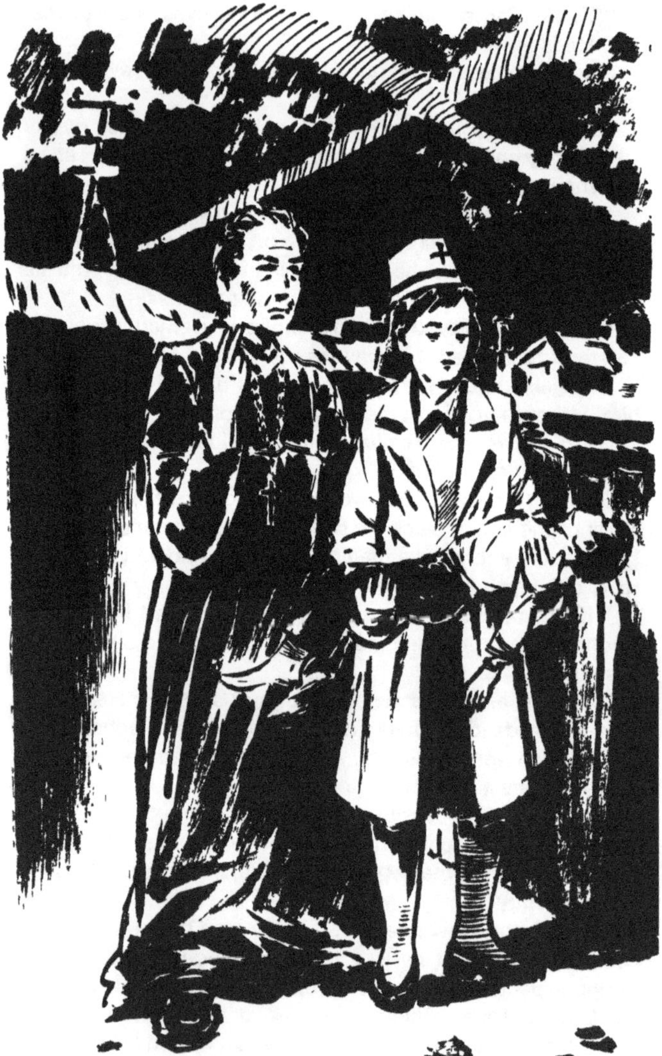

whenever she heard the words that he was a stranger or that he had not been seen these days, everything went dark before her eyes as if she had lost her whole world. She felt dejected as if the sky fell because she knew his personality, his heart, his talent better than anyone else.

They had grown up together in the same neighbourhood.

Hye Gyong's lips trembled as she recalled the song which she would sing with him under the camelia tree in her garden.

> *Camelia flowers, camelia flowers.*
> *Spring goes and autumn comes*
> *But camelia flowers bloom again.*
> *They part and meet again*
> *And always blossom together.*
> *Camelia flowers, camelia flowers.*

In those days they liked to sing this song but they did not understand the meaning. The flowers bloomed and fell several times and she only thought that love meant a pleasant thing. She did not understand full meaning of love and yet she dearly treasured the delight of it. Her teacher mother, from a traditional patriotic family had understood her daughter's mind, but she believed that even in this harsh world the girl would preserve the female chastity symbolized by an upright bamboo with firm roots in the ground. Hye Gyong was well aware of this. But, now that she feared that she might be losing the lover she had held so dear, she was painfully conscious that without him, her youth and beauty would be of little value in this world. It would be useless to have devoted her heart and soul together to academic pursuits pinning hopes on better days.

O Yong Gol went to Seoul to study sculpture two years before Hye Gyong, but he was so hard pressed that he could not pay his tuition fees and had to leave out school halfway through his course. Besides, there had been some family troubles. Around this time, Hye Gyong entered the medical faculty at Seoul University and she was much worried. It was beyond her power to help him financially since she herself was barely managing to study at the university on her mother's meagre salary. She wished to sacrifice herself for him, but she could not ignore the expectation and devotion of her mother who had nobody but her daughter to rely on. Yong Gol's hard plight grieved Hye Gyong deeply. One night he left for home. She saw off her lover and remained for a long time on the platform of Seoul station, feeling lonely and wretched.

From that day on the streets of Seoul looked gloomy to her eyes. It was true that Seoul, which had lost its light and its stability, was an irrational and unjust city where social evils prevailed. And yet, when O Yong Gol was near her, Hye Gyong was not lonely as she felt his warmth and protection. But, when he had gone, she suddenly felt cold as if winter was coming on. But, with unusual tenacity, Hye Gyong had devoted herself to medicine for four years. She went home for every vacation. She could never understand why the train leaving Seoul seemed so slow. Her pleasant expectation of reunion was always marred by misgivings. O Yong Gol was terribly poor. His parents had died long since and he was looking after his younger brother. Yet, in his tiny hut there was always an exhibition of his sculptures in clay and plaster. Once he took up his chisel, O Yong Gol became completely absorbed in his work, unaware of the passage of time. But his eyes began to be lacklustre from disbelief and misery. They said that it was impossible to find beauty in this unjust world.

Hye Gyong, a medical student was very sensitive; she could fathom the heart of the one she loved, by looking into his eyes. His heart was such that he could not still it while there was no freedom, no free air; to live for him was to resist. That was his way of life. Seoul was choking under terrible pressure; the rulers wielded power, and swindlers and imposters swaggered around; debauchery was rife; and there was an ominous undercurrent which might explode at any moment. Walking along the Seoul streets, Hye Gyong thought of her home town, Kwangju, and worried about his lover as if she could hear the beating of his aching heart under her stethoscope.

Each time that she returned to Seoul after a vacation she regretted what she had not done. She knew he needed her caresses, but never once had she embraced him passionately.

Mt. Mudung was radiant in the moonlight, as glittering as if it were covered in countless tiny jades; the guardian of the city, it was also her mountain of love, the mountain associated with their every childhood dream. The town was named Kwangju, "City of Light", because of the brilliance of Mt. Mudung. On every vacation O Yong Gol would take Hye Gyong by the hand and lead her to the mountain. And every time she felt pity for the young man as for a child in need of a mother's embrace. But Hye Gyong ran away from him from tree to tree just as she used to when as children they played hide-and-seek. She laughed and treated his desire as a joke. O Yong Gol complained that she was too cold to him though his sole reason for wanting to go on living in this harsh world was that he loved her. Then she would stroke his wavy hair and whisper: "Please control yourself until I have finished college. All right? You'll be patient and wait, won't you? You'll wait, won't you?"

"Waiting is not the problem. The problem is that you don't love me with all your heart as I do you. You might be right, though. Nobody can tell what would happen to me in this horrendous society. You are free. We had better not take any oath as regards our future. We don't know what will happen to us. I might not meet you again—I might cease to exist at all. Then, when you come to my house, lift the white cover in the corner and you will find a statue into which I put my heart and soul. If you see it, you will understand how much I have loved you and loved living. Though it is not yet finished, it contains my soul. The sculpture will tell you why I won't restrict your liberty and it will show my desire to see you happy. That is the only thing I can give you as a sculptor. This was all I have wanted to say to you. Farewell."

These were the last words she heard from him in her last winter vacation. She did not understand their meaning then. She insisted that he should let her look at the sculpture, but he would not. Educated by the strict mother, Hye Gyong knew that she had to preserve her chastity before marriage, however much she loved him. In order not to cause any misunderstanding, she comforted his heart, his longing for her, with considerate words, before parting. But, once in the train to Seoul, she felt compassion for him, saw how bleak his life was, saw how he was gripped by his desire, his love for her, and looking blankly out of the window, she shed tears.

"My love, be patient and wait just another year. As soon as I finish college, I shall devote myself to bringing your talent into full flower. For me there is no place away from you to live or die. I must be in Kwangju where both of us grew up, breathing the air of the city, smelling the scent of the earth and wood of Mt. Mudung, looking at the mountains and rivers glittering in the moon and the sunlight."

But she had never said any of this in front of him.

When while in Seoul she heard the news that there was an uprising in her hometown, right away Hye Gyong saw her lover's face while his voice rang in her ears. The news of the insurrection sounded like the outburst of O Yong Gol's young heart under an intolerable medieval pressure. Hye Gyong left Seoul Railway Station gripped by anxiety but traffic was paralyzed, and it was not till yesterday morning that she arrived. She went straight to his home. The tiny hut was deserted. With an empty heart she went to her home. She was greeted by her mother and she saw a little boy clinging to her mother's skirt. She hugged the boy and rubbed her face against his. He was O Yong Gol's brother. Her mother gave her the message from O Yong Gol together with the sculpture wrapped in a white cloth. As she unwrapped it Hye Gyong realized that what he had said to her last time was true. It was the statue of a young beautiful woman. She stood firm on the ground, holding high her first baby with her arms, with a smile expressing the joy of motherhood. It also symbolized resistance to fascist oppression, the burning desire for liberty and a bright future. And it had a strong resemblance to Hye Gyong. The face, the eyes, the delicate carriage were all Hye Gyong's. And it was obviously more beautiful and the more real because, permeated with love it held the artist's whole soul. There was an inscription on the base: "To Miss Hye Gyong. I hope sincerely that this smile will stay on your face forever."

Had she read this inscription at some other time, Hye Gyong would have been angry. But, at this moment her heart was torn to pieces at the thought that a tormented noble spirit had treasured and protected her and was now gone forever.

From that day on Hye Gyong joined Kwangju students stretcher-bearing and all the while she searched for O Yong Gol. But she did not find him. Some people told her that a few days ago when the resistance was at its fiercest, he had run

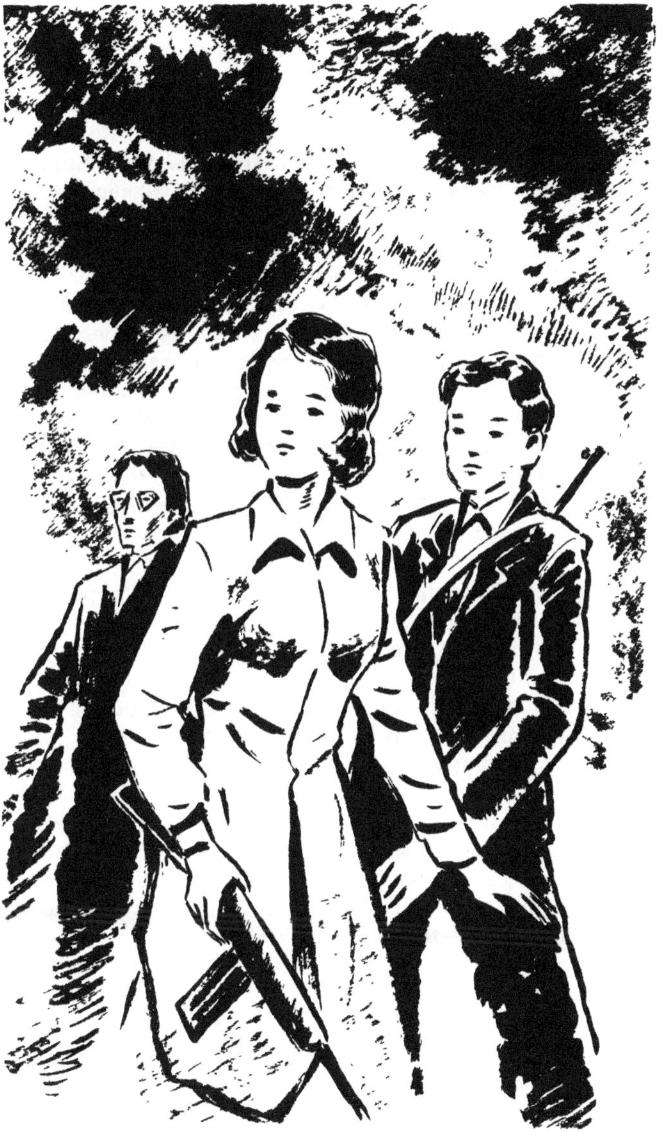

through the streets in a car, a white towel tied around his head, scattering handbills and that with tears in his eyes he was appealing to the townspeople to arise and fight. Others said that the disappearance of this hot-blooded man might mean that he was dead. The reality was too grim for her to live with. She had no courage to open her heart to the priest. But the priest was a man of the world, and in a sympathetic tone of voice he said:

"If I am not mistaken, you are looking for your lover. Listen, girl. Keep calm, when blood is flowing right before your eyes. You must know that a pledge of love may be powerless, because even oaths to God are being thrown aside these days. The last time I saw those notorious paratroopers over there, who committed fiendish atrocities, there were among them some former seminary students who used to call themselves to be apostles of God—dirty Judas-like fellows. Well, that's that. What has happened so far is nothing. Listen to the voices of those fellows howling like wild beasts there beyond the bamboo thicket, by that searchlight. Our town will see more bloodshed, girl."

Hye Gyong watched the searchlight beam glitter past the hem of priest's cassock rustling on the surface of the road. Then, she cried out, "Father, why are you out in the street on this fearful night?"

"Me? I am out to look for people I love just as you are. How can I sit arms folded when the people at the prime of their youth are bleeding and dying? It is my sacred duty as a priest to save them."

The priest looked reverently up at the sky. Several days earlier he had been elected member of the citizens delegation and, ever since, had met the leadership of the insurrection and visited army units and conveyed the demands of one side to the other, in an endeavour to achieve a settlement. However no compromise had been reached. The blood shed by the sons and daughters of Kwangju was dear, and it was too late to negotiate with the military. The priest was going to meet the young insurgents who were defending their stronghold at this final moment of their lives.

"Let us go together, girl. It is likely that the young people who were on Mt. Mudung are gathered where I am going.

How lucky it would be if the young man whom you are looking for is there. Sometimes love is more powerful than the will of God. Nothing would please me more than that such a beautiful girl as you should become an angel who could save those young men and women from the jaws of death. We must join hands and save them at all costs."

The priest looked meditatively at Hye Gyong's face as the searchlight beam flickered across it.

Sometimes the beauty of fair sex is really mightier than the sword, the priest thought to himself. He had an urge not only to help this girl wandering alone through the dark and bloody street in search of her lover, but to get help from her as well.

Hye Gyong followed the priest without a word in the direction of the provincial office square. Sharp horrid sounds came from the edge of the town from where a more powerful searchlight beam was coming, while grim singing voices were flowing out of the provincial building.

> *What we want is freedom,*
> *Freedom, even in our dreams*
> *Freedom to save our brothers.*
> *Freedom, come, come now.*

To Hye Gyong the song was familiar, but her heart was full as she heard it sung. She had been here twice, yesterday and today, but in vain, and she did not pin any hopes on it, she simply had nowhere else left to go. The searchlight slid over the faces of the young men who were carrying stretchers out of the provincial office building. The singing voices coming from the cellar sounded still grimmer, where insurgents were bringing out the bodies of their dead comrades. The city of Kwangju which had been silent as dead, seemed suddenly to begin to breathe.

Hye Gyong ran ahead, but look as she might, she could not find O Yong Gol among the stretcher-bearers, nor on the stretchers, nor among those lying in front of the provincial office building. Three boys carrying buckets and cans of water were following an armed youth through the back gate. The priest had been here several times before, so he was able to take Hye Gyong in through the back gate past the sentry. They followed the boys along the long hallway and went up the stairs to the roof. Hye Gyong was gripped by an indescribably sad feeling and her lips trembled.

The light was dim on the flat roof. Faces were blurred, but they came clearly into view each time the searchlight passed over them, and she lost no time in scrutinizing every face. Some of the men on the roof drank water avariciously from the buckets and cans the boys had brought, and yet they asked the youngsters to go at once, looking angrily at them. Others were practicing their aim, their carbines pointed at the square, and still others extending a fuse of a box of dynamite which would explode when it caught light. Every eye was piercingly sharp. All of them were in the prime of youth. Hye Gyong's eyes expressed surprise mixed with affection. The presence of Hye Gyong in white robe added a bright yet strange tint to the roof this night. Some of the youngsters went on singing, while staring inquiringly at the priest.

"Oh, you lousy guys. Eat the buns. Sing songs after you have reached heaven with Father. Why do you look like that? You'll meet heavenly women there, too."

Hye Gyong was taken aback to hear the burst of laughter intermingled with the familiar dialect of her hometown, but she did not see the face she sought. Again she failed to see the loved face. She was so utterly downcast that she felt as if she now no longer had anything to do in this world. She was at a loss even where to stand.

Presently, a long-haired young man whose head was tied with a conspicuously white towel appeared on the roof, an ammunition box on his shoulder. And, though she could not see his face she knew instinctively that it was him. She felt it, and she knew his smell and breath.

Her breathing sounded louder and her eyes brightened: life had regained its value. She took a step forward to run towards her lover and throw herself into his embrace, with both arms outstretched. But she hid behind the priest and dropped her head and shoulders. He was alive, and she was on the brink of bursting out sobs, but she could not give rein to her emotion, at the thought of the pathetic expressions of the other young people.

O Yong Gol put down the ammunition box by the railing on

the opposite side and was walking over to the priest. The sound of his footsteps was followed by the voice that she yearned to hear. Hye Gyong's heart contracted.

"Why are you here again, Father? We have already rejected these humiliating negotiations that do not begin to meet our demands. Why did you come again? Are you again going to preach surrender? We are tired of such words. Please hurry up and leave here, Father."

"Look, Yong Gol. Why do you talk to the Father in such a way about what is already past? It is not becoming to you," a hefty, energetic-looking man in his twenties, about same age as Yong Gol, who appeared on the top of the staircase interrupted him. All eyes focused on the roof. He must be one of the leaders.

"Father, do not be angry with what he has said. We cannot understand your feeling. Father, can we? We really appreciate that you came to see us. But, Father, I am inclined to repeat what he has just said. This is not the proper place for you to be Father. Please understand that and go back."

The leader nodded his head as if to bid farewell, before he walked to the railing on the opposite side and looked across to the outskirts of the city.

The priest forgot about his companion standing behind him. He was lost in thought. The six young eyes of the boys were also watching his face which glistened every time the searchlight beam slid over their faces. O Yong Gol approached them.

"Why did you come back, boys?"

"We brought some drinking water."

"Splendid. It's all right now. Hurry up and go with the Father."

"What about you, uncle?"

"We'll follow right out. Come on, leave first. Quick!"

Though asked to leave the place time and again, the youngsters would not quit, hovering around the railing.

"Young men," called the priest in a rather austere tone of voice, drawing the attention of all.

"Young men, it is advisable to accept what this old one is suggesting. You are too young to be sacrificed here. What a waste it would be to lose you who have so much ahead. I have consulted with the Presbyterian clergymen of the town, and we both agreed to give you sanctuary in the churches and cathedrals in the town. I want you to leave with me before those devilish packs come surging up here. This is the providence of God, which you must not resist. Come, young men!"

The old priest crossed himself, looking up with his tear-filled eyes at the bluish sky of the early dawn.

A few moments of silence were broken by the voice of O Yong Gol.

"And, you Father! Where in the world are you going to hide our burning hearts and free souls? You'd do better to guide us to heaven. To think of taking us to the churches on earth! Ho, ho...."

O Yong Gol interrupted and stopped smiling, and looking towards the street, he sank into deep thought. He did not bother to look who was standing behind the priest.

The men who appeared to be organizers of the uprising watched the outside of the city where the tenacious searchlight beam originated and had discussions by the railing opposite.

The priest dropped his eyes and became thoughtful as if praying a silent prayer.

O Yong Gol looked at the priest again and called him quietly, bowing his head apologetically, but gradually his voice became harsh.

"Excuse me for my arrogant words. We are young as you said. But, for whom is our youth needed in a country that has no freedom? It is too late. Why are you still talking that way, though you have seen the streets drenched in the blood of the sons and daughters of Kwangju? If we flee from here, it would be a perfidy, a despicable act against our colleagues who shed their blood and fell in the battle for liberty, and against the 800,000 citizens. 'Without liberty it is impossible to love, and if it is impossible to love, we will throw away our hearts.' This is our creed. We may die, but we will defend our human dignity and spirit to the last."

As his voice reached her ears, Hye Gyong was aware that her heart had revived and began to beat again, and she raised her head and tried to go over to him. She thought she had seen new aspects of O Yong Gol's personality which she had never understood before. Just at this moment, by the railing on the far side, someone joined O Yong Gol by declaring: "If we can't speak freely and live freely, we will throw out our tongues and eyes."

All the rest responded by singing in chorus.

> *What we want is independence,*
> *Independence, even in our dreams*
> *Independence to save our brothers.*
> *Independence, come, come now.*

O Yong Gol, pacing over to the railing, joined in the chorus.

Her eyes brimming with tears, Hye Gyong also sang with a clear, resonant voice. Astonished, O Yong Gol spun round, walked over to the priest, but stopped halfway. The priest had clean forgotten about his companion. But when he heard Hye Gyong's voice, he stepped aside. The girl came into full view. Under the dim light Hye Gyong looked at O Yong Gol's flaming eyes and sang with her whole body as if breathing with the song and thinking with the song. The soprano mixed with the sad low men's voices, led them far yonder in the quest for a serene sky where birds could fly and chirp, across the light green grassland and waving ocean, calling and calling for a new world, for reunification.

Hye Gyong's beauty did not lie in her attractive, supple, well-proportioned body or in her graceful, regular face, but in her eyes flashing under her long lashes and her clear, ringing voice. But her beauty was flawless only when her heart beat with that of O Yong Gol. Because, only when she was with him, her eyes shone, her face brightened and her voice was clear and forceful. The young men heard a beautiful soprano join their chorus and perceived her closeness to them. Upon hearing the familiar voice O Yong Gol's eyes flashed with the spark of youth.

"Why, it's you, Hye Gyong. You are here!"

"Yes, it's me, Hye Gyong." The lovers looked into each other's eyes and walked towards each other. As their eyes reflecting the early morning sky met under the dim light, they sparkled.

"Miss Hye Gyong, how did you come to be here?"

"I only arrived yesterday. I have been here many times today."

"While I was in Mt. Mudung, then...."

"I looked for you. Looked for you everywhere," said Hye Gyong, and stared without a word at the broad chest of O Yong Gol for many moments, before she came close to him, her head bowed.

"So you are on such intimate terms," said the priest, delighted. It seemed to him that God had sent a beautiful girl to save the youth. All the eyes on the roof brightened with warmth and watched the reunited lovers. O Yong Gol gently stroked Hye Gyong on the back and lightly pushed her aside and withdrew. At this moment from outside the city there came ferocious voices, sounding like the voices of hungry wolves, their mouths slavering for their prey. The priest approached O Yong Gol and his colleagues who were watching the enemy, leaning on the railing. All the rest of the young men were gathered by the railing, only Hye Gyong remaining in the middle of the roof. Parachutes had landed on the ground beyond the swaying green bamboo thicket. The powerful headlights of army trucks lit on the thicket and the parachutes as if it were broad daylight. A huge group of paratroopers were running wild. Some of them were drinking liquid out of bottles, others brandishing daggers. Their ferocious, brutal eyes glared in the headlights, glared towards the town.

O Yong Gol exchanged a few words with his comrades before he took Hye Gyong hurriedly down the staircase. They sat down on the ninth stair under a carbide light. They did not know that the priest in black cassock had followed them and had halted above them on the fourth step.

"I've longed to see you. How I've wished to see you!"

"So have I!"

"Oh, Hye Gyong, why did you come at this grim hour?"

O Yong Gol patted Hye Gyong's hair with the hand which would use the chisel. His hot breath brought a lump to the girl's throat. The man's eyes sparked for a few moments before they closed as if burnt out.

"Yong Gol, you have lived in this society writhing in too

dreadful an agony for the last few years. Please forget about the pain at least now. Open your eyes and take a look at my face. We are here together now, aren't we? We are together now, aren't we? I'll never go away, I will stay at your side."

Hye Gyong spread her arms and took his hands in hers and looked into his face; then she was about to utter some words as if to throw herself into his arms to form a part of him. She had treasured their love so dearly. They had hesitated to declare their love to each other lest declarations might cool their love. But their reunion would be too short. There was no time. The sound of tanks and loud trucks, loud shots; a deafening roar shook the city; an iron curtain started to envelop it. They felt as if they were down at the hold of a wrecked ship floating in the sea now, instead of in the provincial office. Strangely enough, at this stark moment Hye Gyong recalled the Song of Camelias which she used to sing with her lover in childhood, but her trembling lips prevented her from singing.

"I am ready to stand on the gallows, but my heart weakens at the sight of you. Must I lower my raised head at this grim hour?"

"What are you talking about? I didn't come here to take you away."

"Thank you, Hye Gyong. I promised you the other day. I wished to sculpture your face, your future image vividly, so as to place you at the highest eminence of beauty. But it was not finished. Yet, it is the only work of art that I shall leave in this world. If you perceived the eternal smile symbolic of the future in the statue, I would be happy. This is all the love that I can give you...."

"I saw it. Your work. It has been kept by my mother. She also took your little brother home, too."

"Thank you, Hye Gyong. I have been worrying about my brother, I thank you very much. And the work contains my soul...."

Even at this stern moment, O Yong Gol became livelier and his eyes bright as the conversation turned to art. Hye Gyong was shedding tears now, but he thought of the Hye Gyong of those old days when she was a cute girl whose nose he sometimes flipped.

"Hye Gyong, do you understand what I mean?"

"No, I don't understand."

"Forgive me, Hye Gyong. What could be more beautiful and valuable for us in this world than love? But freedom is more valuable than love. I wanted to live with you for a hundred years but, without freedom.... They are watching us, those who are holding on to this roof. If I prostrate myself under their feet in this land soaked with the blood of my colleagues, how could I be a true son of our Kwangju?"

"You needn't say it, I understand. I understand your heart. And I heard what you said to the Father just now."

"Then do me the last favour," said O Yong Gol, grasping the girl's hands and looking into her eyes. In a broken voice, he said: "Take those children off the roof and leave right now. Hye Gyong, this is love."

The place was narrow and dimly lit, but the girl's burning eyes shot out strong flares. For the first time in her life, passionate words of love flowed out:

"Why do you ask me such a favour? It is too late to do you such a favour.... I have been under your influence. If this sort of thing had happened when I did not understand you as I do, I could have left and lived on in a world without you. But now my heart and body are yours. I'm yours alive or dead."

Hye Gyong preferred to be together with him for a moment, who had protected her purity, rather than to live on sadly all her life seeing the face of the vanquished, of one who had surrendered to the enemy. If she left him and his colleagues, she would be worthless in this world.

"Hye Gyong, our mothers have shed too many tears. Just think of your mother living without you.... And my brother, too.... I can love you only in this way, in no other way."

O Yong Gol dropped his eyes. To him, to love was to protect "You must live on, even though living is harder for you than dying," O Yong Gol said. "When the free society that I and my comrades have yearned for comes to be, you will be happy and so will the children born in this land. I am ready to die, giving my blessings to you and them. That is my will, which you should understand."

Saying this, O Yong Gol wiped the tears standing in Hye Gyong's eyes and smiled.

"Oh, don't talk any more... love is mightier than death, Yong Gol."

Hye Gyong held her lover's head and pressed his face against her pure and soft graceful breast, which nobody but her mother had ever touched, and stroked his wavy hair again and again, for the first and, obviously, for the last time. Her fingers were trembling. Their love facing their last was beautiful, sublime. The priest climbed the stairs up to the roof in deep meditation. They say beauty means a vessel which contains love, he thought to himself. It seemed to him that he had witnessed the existence of pure and clear youth in this harsh world. Death comes to everyone once, but noble love does not come even once to everyone. Their souls blended by a new meaning of life, a meaning that cannot be really understood by people living even a hundred years in tranquility. These souls blended, aspiring across the abyss of death to a free world.

But time was too short. Suddenly a shot sounded. The lovers ran up to the roof. Hye Gyong, standing side by side with O Yong Gol, her white overall fluttering, looked down at the square below. Behind them stood the priest, the skirts of his black cassock waving in the breeze. They could see everything from here. The paratroopers were coming in to occupy the city. The beams of searchlights, headlights and flashlights were sweeping every hidden corner of the street, the street stained with blood in the early morning. Blood-stained daggers glistened, and the slaughter began. There came gun reports, the sound of jackboots, howls and cries and agonized groans. Devilish faces laughed aloud, thrilled at seeing blood spilt by thrusting their daggers into the body of a naked woman tied to a tree. The tanks and trucks which had been running down the street made a halt on the square above which the headlights were crisscrossing. Their bloody eyes were goggling.

This was a confrontation between men and wild beasts. Shading her eyes with one hand Hye Gyong looked down, gritting her teeth. There are no words to describe the eyes of the insurgents about to go into their last battle.

The attackers shouted, "Surrender!", the defenders on the roof responded with rifle shots. The shoulders of the young people holding carbines heaved like waves. They fired in a volley. Below their arms the six boys' eyes twinkled.

"Hye Gyong, this is an order: Take the boys out through the back gate with the Father." O Yong Gol shouted impatiently, pulling the safety pin out of a handgrenade. At this moment Hye Gyong remembered the dead boy she had laid on the flower bed.

"Is it so hard, for a man to live?"

Hye Gyong took hold of the children's hands and looked into her lover's eyes with hers which reflected the dawning sky. She staggered.

"Why, you Hye Gyong.... How come?..." it was a female voice, and all eyes focused on the exit. A woman in white hemp clothes had appeared on the roof. Though no longer young, she has not yet lost her beauty.

She had a striking resemblance to Hye Gyong.

"Mother, why you are here?"

Hye Gyong went towards her mother pulling the children by the hand. O Yong Gol followed.

"You are here, too. And I have been looking for you everywhere.... Oh, Father, how did you get here?" She asked, turning to the priest, who only nodded.

"Mother, please go away quickly and take Hye Gyong. You understand me, don't you? Go right now, please." O Yong Gol took her hand and let go of it before he ran back to the railing and picked up a carbine.

"Please forgive your unfilial daughter, mother," cried Hye Gyong and buried her face in her mother's bosom, before she pat the children's hands in hers. "I can't go here, mother. I shall be with him to the end. I am putting these children in your care, Mother!"

Her mother was struck dumb and petrified. The situation was critical. Yonder, by the railing, a hefty youth held the ignition wire and shook it overhead for the attackers to see.

"Hye, you dogs. Come up if you want to. Then I'll blow up this hall..." the young man shouted—and, clutching his chest, fell.

"Mother, I am medical student. I am supposed to save human lives. How can I leave this place where people are shedding their blood? Mother, please go away quickly with the boys!"

Hye Gyong ran towards the railing. She took a bandage out of her overall pocket, sat down and laying the wounded youth's head on her lap, examined his chest wound with her hand.

"Madame Yong Sun, hurry up and leave with the boys!" urged the priest, pacing restlessly.

"Oh, it seems as if the sky has fallen and the world had turned upside down. Father, how could this ever happen?!"

The mother's lips were trembling, her disheveled hair blowing in the breeze. She was of Kwangju descent; she had lost more than she had even gained. Her father who had been involved in the widely-known Kwangju Student Incident was buried in this land. Her husband who had taken part in a demonstration of Seoul professors during the April 19 uprising was thrown into prison by the military dictatorship, and soon after his release, was also buried in this land. Hye Gyong's mother knew this life and this society well. She had been through it all. She had hoped to live the rest of her life in peace, hoping her daughter might be happy, but her daughter was taking a quite different road from her own.

"Children—my sons, my daughters—come over here. Let me embrace you, for this may well be our last meeting."

She stepped forward with her arms outstretched, and embraced the young people one after another. Lastly she held both her daughter and Yong Gol close and rubbed her cheeks against theirs before she let go.

"Young men" she said, "I did not come here to see you kowtow to those thugs. If you did, you surely could not be the sons and daughters of Kwangju. I wish that I could stay with you to the last, but I am a teacher, so for the children's sake I shall have to go. Boys, we will go first." She staggered down the staircase, holding the boys by the hand. She slipped through the back gate with the children, the young people still calling to her. Having seen the woman off, the priest stood austerely still on a corner of the roof. In the hail of bullets, one by one the young fighters fell. Their blood spread on the roof like a red banner. Presently gunfire eased off.

"Leave here quick, Father," impatient voices urged, but the priest approached Hye Gyong and O Yong Gol.

"I too am a Korean," said the priest. "I have found truth in you. Where could an old clergyman go at this moment, leaving you behind? For a moment, you two young people must stay standing in front of me. You have not been wed, have you? If there ever was anything mightier in this harsh world than the will of god, it would be your love. So please accept, for this is not so much a religious ceremony but my own devotions."

These words were spoken in solemn tones. The priest stroked the young man's and young woman's hair, then, looking up at the sky, crossed himself.

Presently there came bursting, hitting and slamming sounds. The attackers were surging towards the office, their bright bayonets ahead.

Many of the insurgents had fallen and only a few were still alive. Those few formed up around Hye Gyong and O Yong Gol The eyes of Hye Gyong, like those of O Yong Gol, still reflected the morning sky.

"Farewell, Mt. Mudung..."

"Yongsan River ."

"Kwangju River, farewell..."

They formed a circle and called their loved home mountains and rivers Mt. Mudung shone calmly in the early morning light, and below the dark green bamboo thicket swayed in the breeze. The waters of the Kwangju River, and the Yongsan River which meandered through the fertile plain far, far below were calm as ever. The sky above them was too blue and the earth too quiet.

"Oh, where is the spirit of unification?"

"Where is our motherland which will save the brethren?"

They looked over the northern sky with clear, expectant eyes

Meanwhile, the mother who had come out of a back alley with the children stopped at the approach to a bridge. She knew every bridge in the city of Kwangju The attackers were rushing up to the roof of the office A young man grabbed the neck of an enemy soldier and jumped down together, when flames shot up from the roof. Everything was wrapped in the flames, but the uprisers kept on singing

> *What we want is unification,*
> *Unification, even in our dreams.*

*Unification to save our brothers
Unification, come, come now.*

O Yong Gol had pulled out the last round when he collapsed clutching his chest. Yet he was still singing. His headband was crimson with blood. Hye Gyong supported his back with her knees and joined his singing. Her white overall, too, was dyed like a red flag and waving. Now their chorus was dying away. No talented sculptor would ever be able to sculpt their form, yet they themselves formed an immortal statue. Behind them was the priest whose black cassock was wet with blood.

"Hye Gyong, Yong Gol— My son and daughter— I would rather become a stone at your side. Sons and daughters of Kwangju," the mother cried out from the hillock whence she had a good view of the office. Her grey hair was blowing in the wind. And six young eyes beside her were watching.

"My children, don't cry. Look carefully. You must remember these elder brothers and sisters."

The boys stopped crying and looked to where she pointed grim-faced, like grown people, before they climbed up Mt. Mudung, following the mother.